Literature is historic ... aracters who probe or question their faith and/or practices. Corrina Wycoff's clean, spare, thoroughly engaging novel breaks ground in this tradition with fundamentalist Christians. *Damascus House* develops rich pathos for those who choose to cut ties as well as those who remain, while delicately maintaining a focus on the human drama, with neither an indictment nor endorsement of religion itself, except to observe how contemporary people use, abuse, rely on, form identity with, can be disillusioned or buoyed by a man-made institution.

Cris Mazza, author of *Something Wrong With Her* and *Various Men Who Knew Us as Girls*

With the grace of a poet, the calm of an anthropologist, and the urgency of a refugee, Corrina Wycoff lays bare a culture that will be simultaneously shockingly foreign and hauntingly familiar to readers: American fundamentalism. This is an anti-romance, one family's love story with a faith so painful and confusing the only salvation is to break apart everything. An unforgettable novel that will challenge your tolerance and your own capacity for understanding, and ultimately shore up your heart.

Lydia Netzer, author of *How to Tell Toledo from the Night Sky* and *Shine, Shine, Shine*

Without an ounce of sentiment or sanctimony, Wycoff probes the limits of faith, family and love in *Damascus House*. I was hooked from the very first line, as a community of believers is thrown into turmoil. Wycoff writes with authority, precision and a deep empathy that infuses even the most godless of foibles with humanity.

Miriam Gershow, author of *The Local News*

Damascus House

Corrina Wycoff

Spuyten Duyvil
New York City

Acknowledgments

This book is the product of several drafts over the course of just as many years. People have read, commented on, and believed in it during its revisions, and I am grateful to them, most especially to PJ Mark, Duncan McClinton, Deb Olin Unferth, and Deborah Woodard. I am also indebted to the people who helped to shape this book in more elemental ways, especially Mary Brennan, Ron Lee Meyers, Tom Rotolo, and my son, Asher Wycoff. Most, however, I wish to acknowledge my teachers, David Bradley, Ehud Havazelet (in memoriam), and my mentor and friend, Cris Mazza, who will always be the main reason I write.

ISBN 978-1-941550-90-8

Library of Congress Cataloging-in-Publication Data

Names: Wycoff, Corrina, 1971- author.
Title: Damascus house / Corrina Wycoff.
Description: New York City : Spuyten Duyvil, [2016]
Identifiers: LCCN 2015044646 | ISBN 9781941550908
Classification: LCC PS3623.Y35 D36 2016 | DDC 813/.6--dc23
LC record available at http://lccn.loc.gov/2015044646

for the scapegoats

Jesus Knows Your Heart

She had quite possibly just undone her life.

Her husband, Alan, had driven away from the prayer meeting without her, God on his side. Alone, Rachel walked home through Riverview, this New Jersey town where she'd almost always lived. When she was a child and her mother said, "Jesus knows your heart," Rachel sometimes imagined its interior mapped and organized like the town's familiar streets of bungalows and grubby markets. But Riverview in recent years had burgeoned with large homes and stores, and a few blocks from the prayer meeting, a new development of gigantic houses stood. If her parents were still living and if they'd been better with money, they could have put a down-payment on one of these mansions by selling the house they'd bought in the 60s, when land was still rural and cheap. But it was 1995, her parents had been dead for years, and nothing was rural or cheap here anymore.

If Jesus truly knew her heart, she thought, perhaps He'd reveal why she'd just falsely claimed to have aborted a child nine years ago, when she was 17.

She hadn't intended to lie. Hours before the prayer meeting, Pastor Lou had phoned to say that Amy Rotolo had broken her parents' hearts for good and that he'd invited the Rotolos to his house "for food and intercession." He'd said, "You've always been closest to Amy. They'll want you and Alan there to pray with them." As far back as Rachel could remember, her pastor had responded to his congregants' crises with potlucks and prayer. In the mid-1970s, she and the other children from the church—Amy Rotolo among them—would run around the pastor's backyard, catching fireflies, while their parents and the other adults prayed in Tongues over whatever recent abandonment, or illness, or financial catastrophe had inspired the meeting. Some of the adult women, like Amy's mother, would bring tambourines, the men would play their guitars, and by the time the evenings would conclude with the song "I've Been Redeemed," Rachel and Amy would be lying half asleep on the pastor's living room couch, arms wrapped around each other like cartoon bears. Rachel's mother would come in from the yard then, the weather on her clothes, and would lead Rachel outside, into the car, and home to bed.

"I'll bring a salad," Rachel had told Pastor Lou. She thought she knew how the evening would go. Amy had been running away from home since high school; she would have told her parents that their religion was not her own, and she would have announced that she wanted nothing more to do with them, the precise thing she'd done twice before, and which Rachel had asked her never to do again. Then, in a handful of years, she'd get homesick and come back, the ever-prodigal daughter.

Instead, tonight, after the food and before the prayers, Amy's parents disclosed that Amy's departure, this time, was a response to *their* ultimatum.

"Amy's got herself a girlfriend!" Amy's mother had said. "A lesbian girlfriend!"

And Rachel had experienced an odd narrowing of her field of vision. She saw Amy's parents, the other church elders, and the pastor, rigid in their righteousness, talking of Amy's sins. She saw her own husband, Alan, quoting Leviticus. She saw Paul, her high school sweetheart, who'd known Amy as long as Rachel had, keeping characteristically, maddeningly silent. She saw Lee, Paul's wife and Rachel's friend, trying ineffectually to make her small, rational voice heard in Amy's defense. And, on the outskirts of the closing tunnel, it was as though she saw Amy's lovely face, the beloved face whose temples she'd stroked during childhood sleepovers, the face she knew almost better than her own. And, without planning it, she pretended to have done something equally sinful. More than two decades of church membership had taught her that nothing riled the older generation of evangelicals like abortion or homosexuality, and since she obviously couldn't have claimed the latter, she was confessing to an abortion, the sentences finishing themselves before she could even consider what she'd said.

Because her mother had been a Christian and her father had not, Rachel had often struggled to maintain all her loyalties simultaneously. Often, she failed and someone got hurt, but she'd never before chosen loyalty to one over many. Tonight's lie had shown loyalty to Amy, true, but it had hurt the pastor and the members of the church she'd grown up in, to whom she also owed loyalty. Worst, it had hurt Alan, her husband, to whom she owed the most.

She was thinking of Alan, heart hammering with trepidation, as she reached her own neighborhood, where she and Alan lived in one of about thirty cheap, boxy prefabricates circling a rank smelling swamp rumored to contain chemical plant runoff. She unlocked her front door.

"Al!" She hoped to find him in the kitchen, Bible open. They would hold hands across the table and pray together as they always did when, as Alan said, her "walk got shaky." He would pray that she receive God's forgiveness, cast out her spirits, and remind her that Jesus knew her heart. And afterward, maybe he would hold her in their bed and consent to try for a child. But Alan wasn't in the kitchen. The refrigerator hummed.

He wasn't in the living or bedroom, but when Rachel turned on the bathroom light, she noticed vomit in the toilet. This time, perhaps, she'd really done it. Alan had forgiven her indiscretions before. Before he married her, Rachel had confessed to losing her virginity to Paul in high school. Alan had taken her hands in his and had cast out her spirits. "You're new in Christ, Rachel," he'd said afterward, "and I love you in the love of the Lord." But that seemed incidental now. If he believed the lie she'd told, she may have crossed the line separating forgivable from not. She scrubbed the toilet first, then the floor, snagging the towel on the jagged edges of the hastily installed ceramic tiles. She heard the front door open and slam. She was still on her knees, scrubbing, when Alan stood in the bathroom doorway and she turned to regard his wet, red face.

"This is why we can't conceive," he said. "You're accountable for that."

She stopped cleaning and leaned against the cool side of the bathtub, trying to formulate a response. Minutes passed. When she was young, her mother would tell her to "stand in the gap" for her father's salvation, and she would imagine her body stretched like a rubber doll's, one arm and one leg on either side of a great chasm like the one Pastor Lou mentioned when describing the afterworld, sinners and flames on one side and saints and feasts on the other. Half her stretched body reached for her father, who worked so hard and looked so tired, who'd chosen Riverview when Rachel was born because, as he explained, the schools were decent, and he wanted her to have a real future, not a job like his, at the Nabisco plant, which, thanks to their move, he had to drive nearly two hours every day to get to. But the other half of her body belonged to her mother, who wanted nothing more than her father's salvation, who worked as hard praying for it as her father worked at the factory. She would no longer know what to pray and grow silent, and her mother would regard her with alarm, having "received word from God" that Rachel's faith was "lukewarm." She'd say, "You can't hide backsliding from the Lord, Rachel. Jesus knows your heart."

Now, Alan stared silently at her, clearly needing to hear something. The side of the tub grew warm against her back, and she pulled her knees to her chest, feeling her own relative smallness and wondering if Jesus could truly know the heart of something as tiny as she. "Lukewarm," she thought. "Backslider." She wished her mother or her pastor were here, firmly telling her what to say. She wished Alan would tell her. She thought of Amy's face on one side of the chasm. She looked at Alan's on the other. No matter what—if she recanted the lie or didn't—she betrayed someone. "Should we pray?" she asked.

Alan sighed. Wrong answer, then. "I don't know," he said. "I think I need to see the pastor."

"Now?" He'd never left the house so late.

"I just..." Alan said. He looked down at his hands. Rachel noticed his fists clench momentarily. "I just need to pray with him."

She couldn't try to stop him. She couldn't even stand up.

Soon, she heard his car drive away. She didn't know what would happen next. The church didn't permit divorce, but maybe it would in this circumstance. She had no job, no family. She had five thousand dollars of her own. Cast out, how long could that last? All night, the question plagued her. When Pastor Lou phoned at dawn to tell her that he and Alan had spent hours in prayer before deciding on Damascus House, she felt grateful for this new mooring of her circumstances.

"It's a ministry for women who've had abortions," Pastor Lou explained. "You'll be there for a month."

"A month?"

"We're sending you out of love," Pastor Lou said.

"I know you are," she answered.

***

Damascus House stood among Indiana farms and flat brown grasses. Yesterday evening, while Alan and the pastor prepared, she supposed, for Sunday night service, Rachel got off the plane in Indianapolis to find a buxom, waxy-faced woman waiting for her at the gate. This woman somehow recognized Rachel—had Pastor Lou described her?—and waved.

"I'm Grace," she'd said, smiling an audibly sticky lipstick smile. Her name, Rachel decided, was too improbable to be real. "Grace" wore stirrup pants and spangles; her neck boasted a great golden crucifix. She smelled of perfume and warm breath, and her car, a thunderous brown Buick, smelled faintly of dog.

During the drive from the airport, "Grace" explained "the way things work for the girls at Damascus House," beginning with the schedule. Chores at dawn, then breakfast, then group treatment, then a worship service, then afternoon chores, then lunch, then a sermon, then more group treatment, then evening chores, then dinner. After dinner, a repentance service lasted until bedtime. Three meals a day; no snacks. "You won't work in the kitchen the first week," Grace explained. "The first week, you work in the laundry, washing uniforms with the other new girls."

"Uniforms?" Rachel asked.

"Of course! All the girls wear uniforms. Everyone feels more comfortable that way."

The uniform, it transpired, comprised an oversized set of white bloomers, a white undershirt, and a pale yellow jumpsuit suitable for prison. Rachel received the uniform and two white towels upon arriving at Damascus House; in exchange, she yielded her purse—she had fifty dollars in her wallet, for muggers—and suitcase to Grace.

"Don't I get a room key?" Rachel asked.

"It's not a hotel," Grace answered, smiling.

In addition to unlockable doors, Damascus House offered shared bathrooms with no partitions around showers or toilets. Grace showed Rachel: powdered soap for use on both hair and body, powdered toothpaste, toothbrushes (all the same color and small enough for children to use, Rachel noted), and no mirrors. "Vanity is a sin," Grace said, indicating the blank spot over the sink where a mirror would normally hang. "The Lord has shown Father Frank that there's a direct correlation between a woman's vanity and her desire to terminate a pregnancy."

Rachel had been staring at the tiny, identical toothbrushes, wondering whose were whose and whether private toothbrushes were also forbidden here. Upon half hearing Grace's staggering pronouncement, she decided she hadn't listened properly. "A correlation between?" she repeated.

"Vanity." Each word contained the sticky sound of Grace's lipstick. "Abortion stems from vanity."

The following morning, Rachel had still not met any of the other Damascus House residents. But during her designated shower time in the shared bathroom, as she stood brushing her teeth with an arbitrarily chosen toothbrush at the mirror-less sink, one of the others entered. Rachel saw, contrary to her earlier suppositions, that Grace was being neither folksy nor hyperbolic when using the word "girls." The inmate in the bathroom couldn't have been older than fourteen.

"You new?" she asked, barely glancing at Rachel. The girl had a pimply, plump face and a great shock of burned-looking yellow hair tied up in a rubber band.

Rachel regarded the grainy gob of toothpaste she'd just spat into the sink. Yesterday, on the plane from Newark to Indianapolis, she'd eavesdropped on the couple in the seats adjacent to hers. The man had told the woman, "I heard that a new shopping mall opens every thirty-eight hours." The woman, shaking her head, had replied, "That's terrible. That can't be right." They were not much older than Rachel, but, looking at them, she'd imagined they were the kind of adults she herself would most likely never become: adults whose personalities seemed ordered and blunted by savings accounts, small investments, and a working knowledge of things like physics and the opera. They were the kind of adults who seemed to have been adults for a very long time, whereas she still felt subordinate to anyone of her mother's generation at church, and her own inaccurate-sounding age of twenty-six always surprised her.

She looked up from the Damascus House sink and met the girl's eyes. "I'm old," she answered. "Apparently."

"Cripes," the girl said, scanning Rachel's face. "Who sent you here?"

Rachel could not anticipate any conversation that might follow. She understood she'd been sent to a home for wayward girls, and the coming weeks would happen in the lonely company of children. She offered, "Did you know that a new shopping mall opens every thirty-eight hours?"

The girl shrugged. "My mom sent me." Then, without a trace of awkwardness, she undid her uniform and moved toward the showers. Rachel watched the sure movements of the girl's impossibly young body and her own identity seemed to shrivel into a hard little crabapple that rattled, untethered, in her chest.

***

Leslie Manning, "Father Frank's" wife, supervised morning chores in the laundry room. Rachel stood among four teenagers: the yellow-haired girl from the bathroom and three others. One of the others, a girl with a recessed chin, a narrow, slack mouth, and a voice like a hundred metal jacks falling, asked another where she went to high school. "Shut up!" she laughed, "I play against you guys in field hockey!" Meanwhile, Leslie Manning, short-haired and plainly dressed, barked instructions for using a washer and dryer as though no one present had ever encountered such machines before. Rachel, confronting a great hamper of dirty clothes, started separating laundry into two piles. "No!" Leslie Manning said, "No, no, no. You weren't listening. I said to put the yellows in a pile on the right."

Rachel looked down. The whites lay in a pile at her left foot; the yellows, indeed, lay in a pile at her right. She stood still, trying to decide how to fix them.

"The right!" Leslie repeated. And she kicked the pile at Rachel's right foot the merest bit farther. "There," she said. "That's the right."

Rachel stared at her.

"You need to listen," Leslie said. "And you need to remove your piercings."

"My piercings?" Rachel rubbed a finger across a mole on her nose. "It's a mole," she said. "It doesn't come off."

"Your piercings," Leslie repeated. "In your ears."

"Oh." Rachel grasped the tiny diamond stud earrings she always wore. "I don't take these out," she said. "My mother gave them to me the Christmas before she died." She marveled at the story she'd just manufactured. It was Amy's mother, not her own, who'd given her the earrings many years before. This new tendency toward lying alarmed her. She thought of Pastor Lou's sermons about sin, how one sin could open the door to demons, enabling sin to beget sin. She'd never been a liar before.

"You'll take them out while you're here," Leslie Manning said, every syllable stretched out contemptuously. "And that's all of you. We don't mutilate or garnish our bodies here. We are not Jezebels." A long ago conversation with Amy Rotolo stirred in Rachel's memory. Amy had spoken in Jezebel's defense, something about Jezebel's and Ahab's equal holiness, about Jezebel's own piety to the god or goddess she worshipped. Leslie Manning cleared her throat, and Rachel realized Leslie had been standing in front of her, one hand extended, palm up. It must have seemed like a standoff. She sighed, removed her earrings, and relinquished them. "I'm going to check on the kitchen," Leslie said, pocketing the earrings and wiping her palm against her slacks. "I'll be back in fifteen minutes."

"Good thing that lady doesn't have a tattoo," one of the teenagers whispered to another as they all resumed their work. It took Rachel several seconds to understand "that lady" referred to herself.

Leslie did not return in fifteen minutes. Instead, Grace simpered into the laundry room, her perfume overpowering the room's native smells of detergent and hot fabric. She tapped Rachel's shoulder with a long fingernail. "Father Frank is asking for you." Clasping Rachel's elbow, she led her up the stairs to the ground floor. The sour odor of hot cereal oozed from the kitchen.

Father Frank, who was not a priest and who had not, Rachel suspected, been officially ordained by anyplace, met Rachel in the hallway and extended a slender hand. His face, Rachel noticed, was shaped exactly like a peanut, broad at the forehead and chin, but oddly pinched in the center, as though it had a waist. The window of his ground floor office opened onto Damascus House's flat yard where a group of five teenagers in jumpsuits trimmed the low, dry shrubs speckling the property. A sickly taint of sunlight had begun to afflict the lawn, and a hot breeze struggled against the window blinds.

"Have a seat," Father Frank said, the bottom half of his peanut-shaped face expanding oddly when he spoke.

Rachel sat in the nearest chair.

"No," he said. "Not there." He indicated the chair immediately beside the one she'd chosen. It was so close to the first chair that their arms touched. "That's where the girls sit when they come to my office."

"What's the other chair for?" Rachel asked.

Father Frank blinked rapidly. After a momentary silence, he said, "That's my chair." And he sat beside Rachel. She could see his skin's every tiny irregularity.

"So," he said. "I hear that you and my wife got off on rocky footing this morning."

Rachel stared at her hands. What could he possibly think of her, a twenty-six year old woman, sent here? "She confiscated my earrings," she said.

"Leslie wouldn't have done that," he answered, and he placed his large, warm hand on her arm. "You are not the victim. The baby was the victim."

"I shouldn't be here." It seemed crucial to say this. "I don't think my pastor knew exactly where he was sending me."

He nodded and smiled slightly. "You were sent here for a reason. The Lord sent you here for a reason."

"My pastor sent me. My pastor and my husband. I'm twenty-six years old. I don't think they understood."

"What did Paul say about husbands and wives?" Father Frank asked.

"Paul?" What had Pastor Lou told him about Paul? Aside from Amy, Paul was Rachel's only lifelong friend. They'd grown up together in the church before they began dating. It was Paul she'd implicated in her lie at the prayer meeting, while he and Lee, his wife, stared at her, shocked silent. Maybe Paul had joined Alan at the pastor's house later that night? Maybe he had also cast his vote for Damascus House?

"Submission, Rachel," Father Frank said. "What Paul wrote in Ephesians 5."

"Oh." Rachel shook her head. "I thought… Never mind." She wished he would stop smiling.

"The Lord sent you for a reason," he repeated. "We're going to pray." He tightened his grip on her arm and closed his eyes. "Father God," he said, "We come before You with Your daughter, Rachel. We ask that she take this opportunity, Father God, to humble herself before You and before the authorities You've established over her. We ask that she submit, Lord, so that she may be healed." Then, as the prayer reached its crescendo, he placed his hands on Rachel's head and called out, "I cast out the spirits of pride and rebellion Your daughter harbors. I cast them out in Jesus' name."

She'd heard this exact command throughout her childhood, back when she'd stood between Paul and Amy at prayer meetings at the pastor's house. Their mothers, faces lifted toward the ceiling, tears pooling in the corners of their eyes, would lay hands on Rachel and her friends' heads, casting out their demons. It was an act of love, their mothers always said, and they could return that love through their obedience. Rachel would always try to feel the spirits of pride and rebellion leave her body, the spirits, she supposed, that sometimes made her wish her mother would quit the church altogether so her parents could stop fighting, the spirits that made her love her father as he was, saved or not. I will not be proud, she would tell herself. I will not rebel. Afterward, she'd throw herself into her mother's arms, promising to try harder from now on, and her mother would kiss her cheek and say, "Jesus loves you, Rachel."

But Father Frank didn't mention Jesus' love. When, at long last, he finished his prayer with a string of hallelujahs, he regarded Rachel as though rousing from a deep sleep and said, "I sense a strong spirit of rebellion in you."

Rachel felt her head lower automatically, as though in shame. But when she spoke, it was as though Father Frank's accusation had made Rachel even more rebellious. "I'm twenty-six years old," she repeated. "I have a husband. We've actually been trying to have a baby."

The man's smile—that secret, closed smile Rachel feared she would soon associate with her own despair—returned. "If you don't succeed here," he said, "your husband and your church will not be willing to take you back."

Rachel stared at him. Was it true? Could she kneel at Father Frank's feet, humble and undeserving? No, she decided; his response would not be forgiveness or love. He'd probably find a way to characterize even that as a sin, as an act of rebellion. Was rebellion always a sin, she wondered. And before she could fully consider this new thought, she was talking again. “Your wife took another grown woman’s earrings,” she said. “That shouldn’t have happened.”

Father Frank smiled. “It didn’t.”

***

Rachel had barely returned to the laundry room when an instrumental version of “This is the Day the Lord Has Made” sounded over the intercom, signaling it was time to go to breakfast. They would be fed in shifts, Rachel learned; those whose job was to clean the kitchen got their food first, then the laundry workers, then the grounds crew, then finally those who cooked the meal. Looking around the small cafeteria, Rachel saw the house’s population in its entirety: nineteen other inmates, all teenagers. She helped herself to a plastic tray printed with the words “Damascus House: Where lives turn around” and got in line. A girl in a hairnet handed her a small bowl of gray mush. “Oatmeal?” Rachel asked. The girl rolled her eyes. “Oatmeal has too much protein for brainwashing, don’t you think?” Rachel smiled at her; perhaps she’d found someone she could actually talk to here.

She surveyed the four round Formica tables scattered around the linoleum floor, found an unoccupied one and sat, hoping to be joined by the girl in the hairnet. But before she could even bring a spoonful of sticky cereal to her mouth, Grace appeared beside her. "You sit with your pod, Dear," she said.

"My what?"

"Your pod. From the laundry. The other new girls. This table is for the Pod Four girls, when they're done serving breakfast. Your pod's over there." Rachel saw them in the far corner of the room. The blonde girl was talking animatedly to the others.

"My pod," Rachel repeated.

"Yes, Dear. You're in Pod One. Next week, you and the other Pod One girls will be Pod Two."

"Who's in Pod One next week?"

"Whomever the Lord sends." Grace smiled. Her teeth, Rachel noticed, shone brilliantly white.

"There will be more of us next week?"

"No, Dear," Grace said patiently. "Next week, Pod Four goes home. Come on, Dear. Join your pod."

Following breakfast, Grace escorted Rachel and the other Pod One girls to a stiflingly hot second-floor conference room. The other members of her pod chatted together as though they'd always been friends while Rachel stared silently at the wall posters inscribed with basic Bible verses—Joshua 24:15, Colossians 3:20—the very same verses she'd first been made to memorize when she was a child in Sunday School. In those years, she'd repeat them to herself again and again over stale butter cookies and warm fruit punch. Then she'd recite what she'd memorized to her Sunday school teacher—usually Paul's mother or Amy's; the church prohibited Rachel's mother from teaching because Rachel's father wasn't saved. Now, Rachel surveyed the front of the conference room, half expecting to see cookies and punch. The girls continued their chatter, and Rachel deduced the other members of her pod had all arrived earlier on the very same day of her own arrival, and that they all lived locally enough to have been driven to Damascus House by their parents. These post-abortion ministries must exist everywhere, Rachel thought, but only Damascus House, perhaps, was willing to incarcerate an adult.

She could picture the girls' parents, some of whom were probably only ten years older than she, standing in the lobby. The mothers' faces would have been swollen from prolonged hours of tears; the fathers' eyes would have been lowered. The adults would have greeted one another shyly, each suffering the public humiliation that comes to Christian parents who have chosen to disclose their children's sins.

Her own father, Rachel knew, would never have sent her here. His death had shortly succeeded her mother's, but she hadn't mourned it nearly as much. Rachel's mother had once called her father the only man who'd ever made her laugh, but laughter had been quite rare through most of Rachel's life with them. When she was very young, she and her father would go out for dinner once a week while her mother attended an evening Bible study. They'd go to burger places on the highway, places her mother would never have allowed her to eat. Her father called those outings "dates"—a term that made Rachel feel special and much older than she was. Back home, her father would let her watch television with him—scary movies about robots who'd become human or Martians who'd invaded small towns or ghosts who'd taken up residence in people's homes, programs her mother would never have allowed her to see. And even though they'd just finished dinner, they'd eat large bowls of slightly melted ice cream into which her father stirred gobs of mini marshmallows and chocolate sauce. "Kiddo," her father would say as he worked the spoon. "You want some Yabba Dabba Stew?" And Rachel would holler, "Yabba Dabba Stew!" in her best Fred Flintstone. Her mother would return right before bedtime and restore a dreary kind of security with a warm bath, sliced apples, and a Bible story and prayers before lights-out. Then Rachel would lie in bed, nursing a stomach ache and dwelling on the scariest scenes she'd seen on television. She would repress the urge to call for her mother, to ask for comfort. To do so, she knew, would betray her father.

But as she got older, after the "dates" had stopped, Rachel would often come home from school to find her mother crying on the living room couch, a cup of hot tea in one hand, the Bible open on her lap. "He doesn't love us," she would tell Rachel, and she'd repeat her chief complaints—he didn't talk to them, he drank, he watched TV. But most of all, he had no interest in salvation. "Marry a man who loves the Lord," her mother would say. "If he doesn't love Jesus, he won't love you."

Rachel would sit on the floor near her mother's feet and wait for the tears to run their course. Finally, her mother would dry her eyes, offer a watery smile, take Rachel's hands, and say, "This is sin. Let's stand in the gap for him. Let's pray him into the kingdom."

When her father would arrive from work, just before dinner, Rachel would greet him at the door and ask, "Will you come to church with us this Sunday?" And he'd look at her, his eyes tired from his long commute, and answer, "Maybe, Kiddo. We'll see."

But when Sunday came, her father would pretend to be asleep as Rachel and her mother got ready to leave for service, no matter how noisy Rachel tried to be. Or he'd wake earliest and leave the house. One autumn Sunday, instead of coming to church, her father drove to a far away farm to buy fresh apple cider. When Rachel and her mother got home, they found him heating it for them on the stove. The whole house smelled of cinnamon. Services always lasted at least five hours, and Rachel looked forward to liberating her feet from their church shoes, changing out of her scratchy skirt and stockings into soft jeans and a sweatshirt, and padding barefoot around the warm kitchen while drinking hot cider with her parents. She smiled at her father in thanks, but her mother chided, "Apple cider? What good is apple cider going to do you in Hell?"

"I'll throw it on the flames," he answered gruffly. And Rachel, who both wanted and didn't want to laugh, stared hastily at the floor.

Now, Rachel considered one of the conference room posters, which bore the text of Ephesians 6:1: "Children, obey your parents," it read, "for this is right." *But how?* How could she have obeyed them *both*? When "This is the Day the Lord Has Made" played over the intercom again, Leslie Manning, Father Frank's wife, entered. Unfortunately, it seemed that she was to lead Pod One's "group treatment." Leslie closed the window blinds, cutting off even the faintest breeze, then said, "No one touch the windows." She held pencils and paper booklets which she distributed in a crisp, unsmiling manner, as though dispensing bags of food to those she considered heathen. The room's chairs—each with an attached arm desk—stood in a loose circle. Rachel glanced at the packet. The very top of the first page read: "What is Your Spiritual Gift?" Below this question came the subheading: "Is it Prophecy, Teaching, Administration, Exhortation, Service, Mercy or a Combination?"

Each question presented a hypothetical scenario followed by five choices of responses. Rachel's task was to rank the responses; the higher the number, the less likely she'd be to behave in that particular way. "These questions will determine the offices you can hold in the church, according to Paul's letter to the Ephesians," Leslie told them. "Bring your papers to me when you're done."

Rachel was surprised when all but one of the teenagers finished their questionnaires before she had even completed the first page. Perhaps, she thought, they were more accustomed to taking multiple choice tests than she was. She looked at the remaining child, a chubby, olive-skinned girl with a wall of dark, teased bangs protruding vertically from her forehead. With a sudden, overwhelming ferocity, Rachel longed for the trappings of adolescence: deliberate hairdos and timed tests, the presence of a mother who prayed, a father who didn't, and desperate, awkward sex with Paul, fear and shame in the car with them, their inescapable chaperones.

Thank God her mother hadn't been as methodical as Amy Rotolo's. Even though Mrs. Rotolo refused to take Amy to the doctor when Amy got sick or injured, believing, as Rachel's mother did, that seeking a doctor's services demonstrated a lack of faith, she brought Amy to a gynecologist with evangelical sympathies twice a year to have the integrity of her hymen confirmed. "My mom says that God told her I'm sleeping around," Amy explained. Rachel's mother had also threatened that the Lord would enable her to read the sin in Rachel's eyes, and Rachel, uncertain why her eyes still appeared as those of a virgin, always feared the moment God would stop colluding with her and Paul in their secret.

"What if you *do* get a boyfriend?" Rachel had asked Amy. Amy had no idea, Rachel thought, how difficult it was to have a boyfriend without having sex. She and Paul had tried to keep themselves from it. They would just kiss, they'd said. Once or twice, with her mother in the shower and her father asleep in the living room recliner, she'd put his hand up her shirt, and he'd looked nervously at her. But three years after they'd started dating, they'd found themselves alone in a dark car with more privacy than either of them had ever had at home, and it wasn't so easy to stop. "Just for a second," she had begged Paul that first time. "I just want to know what it's like for just a second."

"I won't get a boyfriend," Amy had said.

"'Cause of your mom?" It wasn't because of God, Rachel knew. Though she did her best to pretend at church and only admitted it to Rachel and Paul, Amy had never believed in God.

"Because of me," she'd answered simply. Amy was a genius at secret keeping.

Rachel looked at the girl with the teased bangs and the girl looked back. Perhaps because she'd just been thinking of her, the girl seemed to resemble Amy who, when they were teenagers, would catch Rachel's eye across the church aisles, curly hair teased and sprayed into alarming largeness, eyes occluded. "It's a cult," Amy always said. "You know that, right?" But Rachel hadn't known, and, in fact, still wasn't certain.

During the One Way movement of the 1970s,

Rachel's mother had met Lou Bianchi and his wife, fellow parishioners in the Roman Catholic Church. Soon, her mother, Paul's parents, the Rotolos, and other young families became born-again Christians, left the Roman Catholic Church, and attended the Pastor Lou's weekly evangelical prayer group. The group expanded, filling the Bianchis' living room and finally requiring a larger venue. By 1980, the congregation was large enough to be called a church and met in rented storefronts, then grade school cafeterias, then finally an old farmhouse. In 1985, construction finished on the church's current sanctuary, which stood adjacent to Highway 37 and seated a thousand. At first, the church stood half empty service after service, but in late 1988, after the Rapture scare, and, again, in 1991, after the Gulf War, it filled to capacity month by month. The numbers had dropped in the past four years, but still, on Christmas Eve and Easter—which the church, opposing the Pagan origins of the holiday's name, rechristened "Resurrection Sunday"—it was prudent to arrive an hour early if you desired even standing room at the back of the balcony. It didn't seem like a cult. True, the church's conservatism had grown in proportion to the congregation, until its ideology had become decidedly right-wing. True, the church mandated 10%

tithes from its members, an act verified annually by copies of tax returns submitted to Pastor Lou. True, they were cautioned against making friends outside the church, and dating or marrying an outsider would constitute heresy. And, yes, they had a charismatic leader who heard God's voice and cast out demons. But many of the adults held regular jobs and many of the kids attended public schools, activities Pastor Lou condoned as long as their primary attachments stayed loyal to the church.

And they were loyal, Rachel and her mother. After her mother died, Rachel found boxes in the attic. Her mother had not kept report cards or art projects or awards from Rachel's years in public school, but she'd hung on to every blue ribbon Rachel had ever won at church fairs or Vacation Bible School, every craft she'd ever made in children's church, every Sunday School class photo. In these, Paul always stood in the back row, even though he was quite a bit shorter than most of the other boys, and he never smiled. Even in her new grief, Rachel had found herself laughing when she noticed, in one old photo, that he alone, of all the children, looked dreamily up at the ceiling, strangely unaware of the cameraman's, "Say Jesus!"

She and Amy, meanwhile, always stood next to one another, their outfits coordinated to match.

For two years running, they wore uniforms for the Missionettes, a Christian girls' group meant to offer an alternative to Brownies. When they were in first grade and girls at school began wearing their Brownie uniforms, Rachel and Amy had both asked to join.

"Nothing under the moon could be more wholesome," Rachel's father had said. "Let her be a normal kid for once."

"But she's not a normal kid," her mother had answered. "She's a soldier of Jesus." And she and Mrs. Rotolo had enrolled Rachel and Amy in a Missionettes chapter at the local Assembly of God.

Unlike the enviably fashionable Brownie jumpers, ties, sashes, and knee socks, the Missionettes required pink skirts and white blouses, which each child could purchase anywhere she pleased. "We don't even match!" Rachel complained to her mother after the first meeting, a tedious two-hour letdown that involved repeated singing of "The Lord Told Noah" and "Father Abraham." So Rachel's mother, at the next Missionettes meeting, took measurements for the troop's eight girls, bought a bolt of pink material and Brownie uniform patterns, and hand-sewed matching uniforms, pink versions of the Brownies' traditional attire. Though they both found The Missionettes a fiercely dull substitute for the Girl Scouts, Rachel and

Amy both loved the uniforms, and Rachel learned to sew while helping her mother make more outfits when new girls joined the troupe or current members outgrew or ruined their old ones. Even Rachel's father admired Rachel's mother's handiwork. "You know, they're a whole lot cuter in pink," he said, as Amy and Rachel, grinning, modeled for him. "Brown always seemed like such a funny color to put on little girls. But pink looks really nice. It makes you look like regular, nice little girls."

At school, she and Amy had been learning to square dance, and for Rachel's father, they did their best combination of swings and do-si-dos. "You girls could be sisters, you look so much alike," he said. For Rachel, who was so dedicated to matching Amy that she'd begged Jesus to miraculously loosen her own front teeth when Amy's fell out, just so their smiles would look the same, this was the highest possible compliment.

"It's a cult, you know that, right?" Amy had said. And maybe, to an atheist, lesbian teenager who knew her parents would disown her someday, it really was.

Now, checking off her answers on the Damascus House quiz, Rachel wished she'd been years and years older than Amy. Amy would have been well served if someone had taken her side years ago. If Rachel had done it then, perhaps Amy wouldn't have ever needed to run away. Or, more importantly, she wouldn't have ever needed to come back.

Amy first ran away during their sophomore year of high school. Her parents found her within a week and brought her home. In college, she disappeared again, this time for three years. Amy's parents had sent her to a prestigious, secular girls' university, a decision about which Rachel's own mother said, "I love the Rotolos, but they're letting their pride get in the way by not sending Amy to Christian school." And Rachel felt the resurgence of a childhood dread, her old worry that God might disclose Amy's atheism to the Rotolos, the pastor, or to Rachel's own mother. Rachel's friendships with non-Christians were relegated to school property and special occasions. If Rachel asked to even walk home from the school bus with the neighborhood's non-Christian girls, her mother would say no, quoting, "Be *in* the world, not *of* it," and Rachel would worry that, eventually, her mother might prohibit her friendship with Amy. Still, that summer before college, she sometimes pretended that she and Amy were finally old enough to be permitted to make their own choices.

All that fall, Amy and Rachel talked on the phone every day. Amy even flew, twice, to spend weekends with Rachel in her dorm at Maranatha College, where they shared the little dorm room bed. Over Winter Break, Rachel designed and made each of them dresses for Christmas, which they wore to the candlelight midnight service on Christmas Eve, where Amy's mother raised an eyebrow and said, "What's all this business with her neckline, Rachel? Why is she showing so much décolletage?"

"Décolletage?" Rachel mouthed silently, and Amy laughed so hard she lost control of her candle, dripping wax all over Paul who lurked awkwardly nearby and with whom Rachel had recently broken up. Amy had been the one to listen to her through that break-up, night after night on their respective dormitory telephones, both of them running down their calling cards so fast that their mothers insisted they get part-time jobs after the holidays to subsidize this expense.

But Amy phoned less frequently when they each returned to their schools after New Year, and when Rachel would call Amy's dorm, her hallmates would yell and yell her name, sometimes returning to the phone to tell Rachel she wasn't there, sometimes leaving the receiver unattended until Rachel hung up. Then, at Spring Break, instead of coming home for Easter, Amy sent her parents a letter, saying she'd decided to drop out of school, to move away from her college town, and to start working full-time instead. Amy would move to Oregon, her letter said, but it didn't name a city. The Rotolos were hosting Resurrection Supper that year, and Mrs. Rotolo cooked and cleaned and baked, though, at dinner, neither she nor Mr. Rotolo ate anything, and Rachel, who could not yet understand what Amy had done nor why, watched them sadly. "She didn't tell me," she assured them again and again. "I don't know why she didn't call me."

Back at school, Rachel, without both Paul and Amy, feeling lonelier than she'd ever believed possible, prayed for a new best friend. Days later, she saw a help wanted sign posted in the window of the campus tea shop and, shortly after being hired, met a girl named Lee, whom she quite immediately loved.

"God doesn't answer my prayers too often," she told Lee, once they'd become friends, "but He sure did with you."

And Lee had laughed a great, flattered laugh, just as Amy would have.

When, after three years, Amy started visiting her parents again and Rachel could finally ask her why she'd left, Amy only answered, "Religious freedom. Same reason the Pilgrims left England."

"But why cut ties completely?" Rachel asked. "It's so extreme."

"Extreme?" Amy laughed. "But casting out children's demons isn't?"

Yes, Rachel admitted. That was extreme, too. And she told Amy about her own religious double-life—her doubts about Heaven and Hell and the apocalypse, and the fact that, unlike just about everyone else from church, she'd never once heard God tell her anything. Still, she explained, a little bit of pretense, for the sake of obedience, made sense.

"It wasn't just a little bit, though," Amy said. "I was lying all the time. I hate that I'm doing it again."

"Well, if you do decide to disappear again," Rachel said, "don't stop talking to me."

Amy looked at her with bright eyes and kissed her forehead. "You could come with me."

"I can't," said Rachel. Her mother, then, was still alive.

"I know," Amy said. "You're not the one living a lie."

Now she was, though, Rachel thought, as Father Frank's wife read her answers and calculated her score with a stubby pencil. "Your gift is exhortation," she said crossly, as though Rachel did not deserve even the barest trace of civility. "So you really need to get over the attitude you came in with."

"What do you mean?" Rachel asked.

"Oh," she said, her voice much gentler. "Exhortation… let's see." Rachel had the sense Leslie was groping for the smallest possible words.

"Not the definition," Rachel interrupted. "What do you mean about my attitude?"

"That's what I mean," Leslie snapped, her patronizing sympathies quite dissolved. "Exactly that. You're our senior resident. You need to motivate the younger girls."

"I shouldn't be here," Rachel said again. "It's a mistake."

"The Lord's the expert," she replied, "not you."

***

The worship service followed; all the prisoners crowded into a chapel room at the back of the building. It was a plain chapel, rather like one Rachel would have expected to find tucked away in an airport or a hospital. Sometimes, in dreams, she took refuge in such rooms—secret, solemn places she happily discovered in dark, chilly hallways of eerie old houses.

Father Frank assumed the pulpit and began to pray. "Your daughters are here, Father God," he said, "to repent for the murders of Your beloved innocents, to beg for Your forgiveness, and to go forth, cleansed in Jesus' blood, to live without sin forevermore." The lights dimmed, and a movie screen lowered behind him with a gentle whir. They would sing soon, Rachel thought, and lyrics would appear on the screen. At Pastor Lou's church, after the screen fell, the music ministry always assumed their places at the altar and began to play songs Rachel had known all her life, the lyrics on the gigantic screen behind them, for newcomers. The congregation would sing in English and in Tongues. Sometimes the men, allegedly overcome by the Holy Spirit, would rush into the aisles, jumping and hugging and laughing. Whenever Alan joined them, Rachel watched his face brighten with joy and thought of her own father, wishing he could have had this happiness, too, and worrying that her own evil spirits of pride and rebellion truly could have prevented his salvation.

Is rebellion always a sin? she thought again.

As if in answer, the Damascus House screen brightened, not with lyrics but with an enormous red and pink photograph. Rachel needed several seconds to identify the image as an enlarged, mutilated fetus. A crucifix hung on either side of the screen, each adorned with a grotesquely bloody icon of the dying

Jesus. Soon, another screen-sized image—the fetus sliced and ravaged—replaced the first. For a moment, Rachel and the Pod One girls were united, staring relentlessly at the carnage. "Oh," said the yellow-haired girl from the bathroom, and her eyes revealed she'd connected to some previously untapped inner horror. Meanwhile, Father Frank had lighted upon one scripture, which he repeated with increasing volume. "Vengeance is Mine, sayeth the Lord," he said. "Vengeance is Mine."

He circulated among them, repeating the scripture, placing his hands on girls' heads. A girl in the row in front of Rachel—perhaps she was in Pod Two?—fell backward when the pastor touched her. As he moved down the rows, the other girls fell, too, collapsing onto their chairs via a process those in Pastor Lou's church referred to as "falling slain in the Spirit."

Rachel loved this phenomenon at her home church, but it frightened her here. Amy, she remembered, blamed falling slain on mob psychology at times she seemed to be feeling generous and on hypnosis at times she seemed not to be. But Rachel had often fallen slain and she'd never felt in the thrall of hypnosis nor mob psychology. She'd merely felt Pastor Lou's hands on her head before her knees gave way and she tipped slowly backward, unable to stop. At her church, no one crashed onto chairs as they did at Damascus House. Instead, male ushers caught the falling parishioners, lowering them gently onto the floor. Immediately afterward, female greeters draped cloths over their laps or legs, for modesty's sake. Lying on the cool floor, the cloth over her legs, Rachel would pray for a vision, like the ones her mother, and, these days, Alan, always received. But, getting none, she'd sometimes fantasize about her parents laughing with one another or sharing a kiss; or, in later years, how she and Paul might be able to sneak off in the car later that night; or, most recently, that Alan might do something other than roll roughly atop her for a few minutes in the dark, that he'd let her press against him with the lights on, or kiss her hairline, or undress her slowly. Always, though, ashamed of her carnal, backslidden thoughts, she'd silently repent.

"Vengeance is Mine, sayeth the Lord," Father Frank continued. He had arrived in Rachel's row. Rachel watched the blonde girl fall, her face crumpled and tense, like a toddler's. "Vengeance is Mine," Father Frank shouted as he grabbed Rachel's head. And as though the spirit of rebellion rose inside her again, she decided she would not fall. Not here. "Vengeance is Mine, sayeth the Lord!" He repeated the verse more and more loudly, but Rachel remained adamantly on her feet. All around her, the girls who'd fallen began to rouse; their voices obliged the pastor with shouts and sobs of "hallelujah." Father Frank looked at her through narrowed eyes and pushed against her head with what must have been his full strength. Rachel lost her bearings and toppled backward, stumbling over one of the Pod One girls who'd managed to stand halfway up, and landing painfully. Her elbow and lower back throbbed and little specks of glittering light swam in her vision. "Don't help her," Father Frank's wife, materializing from somewhere, told the other girls as Father Frank moved back toward the pulpit. Meanwhile, it was as though Rachel could hear Amy Rotolo's long ago voice. It said, "Remember, kids, every time you sin, God kills a puppy!"

***

The day's events repeated with small variants to help one mark whether it was morning, afternoon, or night. The sheets they'd washed in the morning were clean and dry by afternoon, and it was time for the Pod One girls to put them on the stripped beds and to clean the house's tiny bedrooms with dust rags and carpet sweepers. Lunch, a scandalously small offering of instant noodles, preceded another tortuous round of group treatment during which Father Frank's wife told the Pod One girls to write letters of apology to whomever they'd most hurt by getting abortions. She passed around lined, white paper and freshly sharpened pencils. Rachel wondered which pod held the responsibility of pencil duty.

"Can we write to the baby?" one of the girls asked. She raised her hand first, as though in school.

"Write to the living," Frank's wife answered. "The baby belongs to Jesus now."

Rachel thought of Alan. He'd probably gone to church after his long workday and, this moment, knelt at the altar, praying for a fetus that never existed. Again, she considered confessing that she'd lied. But he would be sure to tell the pastor, who would, in turn, tell the Rotolos. She could almost see Mrs. Rotolo's relieved face, her anger with Amy newly cemented, as though Amy were the only one who'd ever sinned. She wrote: "Dear Alan, The Lord said that only one without sin can cast the first stone. The Lord has forgiven me. I hope you and Pastor Lou can forgive me too." She brought the letter to Frank's wife, as instructed.

"Give me your pencil," she commanded, and when Rachel obeyed, erased everything other than "forgive me." Then she handed the paper back to Rachel and ordered, "Try again."

Rachel resumed her seat. She'd begun dating Alan at a vulnerable time. She'd graduated college the previous June. Her mother had chosen Maranatha College because it still offered a major in Home Economics ("It's practical *and* scriptural!" her mother had said, thrilled.) Then, just months after graduation, after Rachel, Lee in tow, had returned to Riverview and had tried to find any job outside of waitressing for which her "practical" degree qualified her, her mother died. It was a sudden death, and neither Rachel nor her father was at home. Rachel had been out to breakfast with Lee, ordering biscuits and gravy with sides of sausage and bacon, just to goad her vegetarian friend. "So good," she'd told Lee, waving a bacon slice.

"You probably don't even like it," Lee had laughed. "That's the truly obnoxious thing about what you're doing."

Meanwhile, her mother had felt pains in her chest and her arm and had called Pastor Lou for prayer rather than a doctor for treatment. By the time the pastor and his wife had gotten to the house, her mother was dead. They called paramedics and followed the ambulance in their car. When Rachel finally arrived at the hospital, her mother's body had already been moved to the morgue. It seemed impossible the day could have begun with biscuits and gravy.

That night, at least three dozen church members convened at the pastor's house. Rachel's father hadn't wanted to go, but Rachel had begged him. She knew it was where her mother would have wanted them to be, and she couldn't bear to disobey. Her father stayed in the pastor's study, the door closed. When she went to check on him, she found him sitting at the pastor's desk, bending and unbending a paper clip.

"You OK, Dad?" she asked.

"I have no idea," he said, his voice thick from silence.

Rachel lay on the pastor's worn leather couch, her shoes on. They didn't speak. She thought of colicky babies she'd seen in the church's nursery, their little, hurting bodies rigid. She could hear the pastor leading the others in prayer in an adjacent room. Without her mother, she didn't know how to finish the prayers she started.

It was very late when the study door opened. Pastor Lou and his wife, Amy Rotolo's parents, Paul's parents, and Alan crowded inside, their faces pale. Lee and Paul stood in the hallway.

Pastor Lou crouched beside Rachel's father, his head only slightly higher than her father's knees. Rachel wasn't listening as Pastor Lou began to talk of Lazarus until he said, "Some of us have received word from the Lord that I've been anointed to bring your wife back." Rachel lifted her head and held the pastor's gaze. She thought again of the nursery at church, a large basement room where mothers could leave their infants in the care of other women so as to attend service undisturbed. Each mother was given a number on a slip of paper. If her baby grew inconsolable, the nursery workers would project that number onto a small screen at the back of the sanctuary, signaling the baby's distress, and its mother, seeing it, would decide whether to attend to her child or whether to let the nursery workers try to soothe the baby instead. Rachel had never wanted to believe that her father would go to Hell and had, therefore, never been able to fully believe in Heaven, but her insides roiled with hope and horror as she envisioned her own mother in an enormous heavenly sanctuary, seeing her number on the screen.

Amy's mother, looking at Rachel and at Rachel's father in turn, challenged, "You both need to stand in faith with us if you want for this to happen."

But Rachel's father, the veins in his red hands bulging, catapulted from the desk chair. Amy's mother looked so small beside him. "What are you people?" he hollered. "Imbeciles? What are you, a pack of dogs? She's being embalmed! A pack of dogs would know that." He turned toward the pastor. "Please," he said. "Have respect. All these years you took her from me. Let me say good-bye without a circus."

"Dad," said Rachel.

"No more." He shook his head. "I'll see you at home."

In the immediate silence that followed her father's departure, only Alan seemed to notice her. Paul and Lee whispered together. The pastor and his wife attended to Amy's mother, who seemed to be mourning harder than everyone else. And Amy's father was standing with Paul's parents, casting concerned glances at his wife. But Alan approached, placed a hand on Rachel's shoulder, and said, "The pastor forgets that we're in the last days. Lazarus wanted to come back. But your mom's not sorry she joined Jesus a little early. We won't have to miss her for long." Like Heaven and Hell, the End Times story was something Rachel could not believe while staying loyal to both her parents—even their deaths hadn't changed that—but it was still the kindest thing anyone could have said, and she'd nodded gratefully.

Rachel lived alone with her father, moving through the empty house, grappling with the days and days of quiet. She'd hung photos of her mother in every room. "Where are you?" she'd ask the photos, while her mother's face smiled enigmatically. Even though it felt disloyal to her father to admit it, she understood the pastor's wish to bring her mother back. At first, her mother's death felt reversible, the way locking keys in the car feels, in that split second between doing and done. During the first few months after her mother died, Rachel often locked her keys in her car. At church, she mentioned how frequently she'd been calling locksmiths, and Alan asked her to make a spare key for him to hold. He'd rescue her with a hug and say, "Jesus loves you, Sister." Eventually, he began to bring her a flower whenever she'd call, a Bible verse, neatly printed, attached to the stem. One early spring day, in the pouring rain, Alan met Rachel in the parking lot of the restaurant where Rachel waited tables, spare key in hand, and the verse on the card he'd attached to the flower—he knew, by then, that daisies were her favorite—was from Psalm 42: "Why are you downcast, o my soul? Put your hope in God, for yet I will praise Him, my savior and my God." And without having planned to, Rachel kissed him, their lips, already wet from the rain, utterly without traction.

At home after work, Rachel would do the housework and cooking for her father. On Wednesday nights and Sundays, she and Alan would go to church together.

She knew she should try to bring her father along, that it's what her mother would have wanted. Amy's mother often reminded her of this, that even death should not stop a child from honoring her mother. But the commandment, like the scripture hanging in the Damascus House conference room, ordered children to honor *both* their parents, and Rachel wasn't sure how dragging her father to a church he detested and blamed could possibly qualify as honoring him. Still, one night, not long before bed, she approached him in the living room.

"You want some Yabba Dabba Stew, Old Man?"

He smiled at her. His teeth had changed a lot, she noticed. They were stained, as though he'd stopped brushing them. He was watching a game show, the television volume muted. "You want to sit down?" he asked. He was stationed in his recliner, his bare feet resting on the ottoman, his heels a mess of cracked calluses, his toenails long and ragged.

Rachel sat on the couch. On television, a slim contestant dressed head to toe in chocolate brown cheered silently over her winnings. The living room clock ticked. When she was little, she heard, "Jesus, Jesus, Jesus" in its rhythm. She remembered how her mother had hugged her when she'd pointed this out. She looked at her father. What would it have been like to have been married to someone who spent all her time praying for your salvation, but not a single moment talking to you? She had never seen her parents kiss. She had never seen them hold hands. Her mother had sacrificed her whole life for one prayer, Rachel finally understood. She had sacrificed even the very thing she was praying for.

She had to try.

"Mommy wanted you to be saved, Daddy," she said. "It was the only thing she ever wanted."

"Oh, Kiddo," he sighed.

"I love you, Daddy," she said. "Jesus does, too."

"That's good," he said. "About you, I mean."

"What about Jesus?"

"Please, Rachel," he said. "Your mother's gone. Leave it be."

Only months later, he died of cancer no one knew he had. Stunned, Rachel sometimes comforted herself by picturing an afterlife different from the one described at church. She remembered Amy Rotolo saying, "With all the sacred texts in the world, how could only one be right?" Perhaps her father had been reincarnated, Rachel thought. But she remembered her mother, encountering Rachel, Amy, and Paul watching a cartoon version of *The Ramayana* they'd happened upon after school one afternoon, snapping the television off and shouting, "Stupid, Satanic religion. Stupid, Satanic reincarnation. Why would they broadcast this?" And, guilty, she'd instead try to persuade herself that her father had secretly asked for salvation in the very moments before he died. But the pastor, Paul's parents, and Amy's mother shook their heads when she proposed this idea at a prayer meeting. "He died in sin, Honey," Mrs. Rotolo said. "And the Lord's going to hold us all accountable for it."

"But only Jesus knows our hearts," Rachel argued. "You can't be certain that he died in sin."

It *was* certain, however, that he died in debt, and Rachel got nothing, not even the house. In two months' time, she would have absolutely nowhere to go. But there was Alan. Of all the people from church, he alone helped her box her parents' belongings, selling whatever could be sold, storing, in his own house, whatever she wished to keep, and donating the rest. He alone brought her dinners he'd prepared, saying, "I hate to think of you eating all your meals at work." And when she'd try, sometimes, to kiss him, he'd stop her, saying, "I don't want to take advantage." He cared for her. He owned a house. He loved the Lord.

Rachel stared at the lined paper in front of her. "I was lost when my parents died," she wrote. "You were the only one who cared. I'm sorry. Please forgive me."

"Better," Father Frank's wife said, reading the new letter. And she placed it in an envelope which she sealed with her flat, surprisingly large tongue.

***

When the mutilated fetuses appeared on the screen during the day's final service, the Pod One girls seemed inured to the images, even though the Damascus House staff played a new hand by alternating them with photos of fat, living babies. The service's content varied only slightly from earlier in the day. Father Frank talked of repentance and vengeance, some girls prayed and fell slain, and the gore flashed on the screen. This is all they have, Rachel thought as Grace led the Pod One girls to bed past midnight; this is their full arsenal.

The bed they'd provided was overly hard and the pillow was not hard enough, so, tired as she was, Rachel could not sleep. No air managed to find its way through the room's singular, small, high window. "You're our senior resident," Father Frank's wife had said. "You need to motivate the younger girls." What in the world would the gift of exhortation look like in this situation? She thought of Moses, of Jacob's son Joseph, of Daniel, and of Abraham. She wished she could be visited in the night by a dream that inspired, frightened, and made correct courses of action divinely clear. She closed her eyes. She wished for everything. She wanted to pray, but prayer made no sense at Damascus House. She wondered if Father Frank knew that. "Vengeance is Mine, sayeth the Lord," he'd said.

Too bad vengeance wasn't a spiritual gift, Rachel thought. It would be much easier to succeed at vengeance than at exhortation sometimes. That was why, she realized, she'd told everyone about the imaginary abortion. Vengeance, she finally understood, was the darker side of loyalty—and she hadn't acted out of a singular loyalty to Amy, as she'd previously thought. Yes, out of loyalty to Amy, she'd wanted vengeance against the Rotolos. But, out of loyalty to her father, she'd wanted vengeance against the pastor and the others.

And, perhaps most of all, it seemed to her now, she'd wanted vengeance against Paul.

When they were little children—just four or five years old—their mothers had told them they'd get married someday. They were raised to be obedient, so they'd repeated their mothers' promises. Before she left for college, she'd even begged him to follow her, but Paul's parents had already planned that he'd take over his father's stores, and he was too obedient to do anything else.

"I'll wait for you," he promised her.

During her first months at college, she learned to knit and began to make Christmas scarves for her parents, Amy, and Paul. Her father's would be blue and green, her mother's yellow and orange, Amy's, a raucous pink. But she didn't know what color Paul might like. She couldn't even begin to guess. And the more she thought of him, the more she realized how little she knew about who he was. She'd always been the one who did the majority of the talking, the one who'd had friends and interests and ideas. Finally, one November night, as she sat in her dormitory hallway on the phone with Paul, she'd asked, "What's your favorite color, anyway?"

"I don't know," he'd answered. "I probably haven't thought about it since kindergarten."

"What was it then?"

"I don't remember," he'd said. "I bet my mom would know."

It wasn't long afterward that she asked him to stop waiting for her.

When she started working at the tea shop, Rachel had an excuse to stay at school during some holidays and summers, and when her mother would ask, "What about Paul?" she'd recite a phrase she'd often heard her mother use: "I'm waiting for some direction from the Lord on that."

Rachel was obedient, too, of course, and acquiesced to her mother's insistence, after college, that she move back home. The war in early 1991, just years after the latest Rapture scare and months before Rachel's college graduation, inspired her mother, like many from the church, to expect the Rapture sometime soon. "These are the End Times," her mother said. "If the millennium starts in 2000, then Tribulation starts in '93. You need your church." Rachel waited for her mother to ask about Paul, but on that first Sunday back in church, she pointed to Alan instead, hinting, "Remember what a skinny thing he used to be? Look at him. These times call for men on fire for God. And Alan loves the Lord." Rachel had grinned with relief. After service, she saw Paul across the sanctuary. He smiled at her and waved, and, overcome with guilt, she decided to introduce him to Lee.

So he became poor Lee's problem. Lee had been such a solitary little thing when Rachel first met and loved her. Whenever Rachel talked about Riverview, her lifelong church, her parents, Lee would stare hungrily. "I don't have anyone," she said. "I've just aged out of the system." It was a phrase Rachel had never heard before. She thought of kids from the city—charity kids—who'd come, every summer, to stay with families from her church, to swim in the ocean and play in the sand. It seemed natural to bring Lee to Riverview. Her mother called Lee, "Rachel's skinny stray," and Lee fit the part, trailing Rachel everywhere and wearing her clothes, the little sister Rachel had always wanted, a younger version of Amy Rotolo, one who'd never leave. Sometimes, when they walked together in a store or through the neighborhood, Rachel would look at Lee's small face and haphazard brown curls, and, overcome with affection, take her hand.

When, after three years of being away, Amy Rotolo finally came back to visit, Rachel worried that Amy and Lee wouldn't like one another, that she'd have to choose between them, but they all stood in the park like teenagers, Amy smoking cigarettes end to end, and Rachel, delighted to see them getting along, even allowed them to talk about the scriptures, letting Amy use the Bible to defend her atheism for nearly half an hour before asking her to stop.

"Rachel's a believer," Amy told Lee, smirking.

"I try to be," Lee replied. "I talk to God all the time. I just don't think He hears."

"Well," said Amy, "maybe there's something to predetermination, then."

"And He picked *your* mom?" Rachel laughed.

"We basically have the *same* mom," Amy said. "You just don't notice because you're a better daughter. Maybe our moms are God's type."

"He didn't pick me," Lee said.

"You're too insecure for salvation," said Amy.

"Yes," Lee agreed. "Aren't you?"

Amy shrugged. "It's more like I can't believe there's anything up there caring about these little things people think and do."

Rachel's father had often voiced this perspective, too, and Rachel weighed it against her mother's, wondering whether she preferred being watched every minute by a god who knew everything she did, good and bad, or being watched by no one at all.

"Who loves us if no one's watching?" she asked.

"No one does," said Lee. She was wearing Rachel's shoes.

"We love each other," said Amy, lighting another cigarette. "If we're lucky."

Lee paused. "That guy Paul, your ex? He's cute."

"Paulie?" Amy laughed. "He looks the same as he did when he was six."

"He's a child," Rachel agreed. Then she giggled. "I've seen his weenie."

"Who hasn't?" Amy added quickly. "We all took baths together as kids." Later, Amy would tell Rachel to be careful. Lee was desperate to belong somewhere, she explained. "You have to protect your secrets," Amy said. "Who knows what she might repeat someday?"

Then, only weeks later, Rachel's mother was dead and there were no more secrets to keep from her. Soon, as Rachel had hoped, Paul and Lee were together, and Lee was positioned to finally have both family and home. So, when Alan proposed marriage by detailing his plan to become assistant pastor and the *agape* love he would need from a wife—the kind of love, he said, they already felt for one another—Rachel accepted. They married almost immediately—a tiny, early afternoon ceremony in the sanctuary, attended by fifty of the longtime church members, officiated by Pastor Lou, and followed by fancy cookies and finger sandwiches in the all-purpose room in the church basement. Rachel wore the same dress—a plain, white cocktail-length affair she'd designed and made herself—that she'd wear, a month later, to Paul and Lee's bigger, more expensive wedding. She wore delicate silver shoes and curled her hair. She had no maid of honor, and Alan, looking handsome in his best Sunday suit, had no best man. At Rachel's insistence, she and Alan approached the altar together from the church's front pew, so she wouldn't have to walk down the aisle toward him, no father by her side. When it was Lee's turn to get married, Rachel insisted that Alan escort Lee down the aisle, and Alan, whom Rachel still regarded as her best ally, agreed. It seemed, then, as though Rachel and Paul's adolescent romance had vanished from everyone's history, just as something heavy could fall through the surface of the sea and leave no mark at all.

Nearly three years had passed since those weddings, Lee and Paul had already had a child, and Amy Rotolo, after visiting often enough for Rachel to almost stop dreading her next disappearance, had finally vanished again. "You were always closest to Amy," the pastor had said the night of the prayer meeting. "The Rotolos will want you there."

But the Rotolos hadn't yet arrived when Rachel and Alan entered the pastor's house, where Paul's mother and Pastor Lou's wife stood drinking iced tea at the kitchen counter, and where Paul and Lee's precocious two-year-old, Justine, worked a fat magenta crayon industriously across a coloring book page at the kitchen table.

Lee, who'd been fussing with a plate of crackers and cheese, arranging and rearranging rows, practically ran to Rachel and took her arm. "Paul's mother brought Jussie that coloring book," she said. The page Justine worked on, Rachel could see, told the Bible story of Jacob who labored seven years to earn his beloved Rachel in marriage but was tricked into marrying Leah, Rachel's older sister, instead. Later, he was given Rachel too, but another seven years was added to his indenture.

"Look," Lee said quietly. "Look at the caption."

Below the picture of a woman in long robes, holding a baby, the text read, "And Leah thanked God and said, 'Surely the Lord blessed me with this child because He knew my husband hated me.'"

Lee's grip tightened on Rachel's arm as she led Rachel away from the kitchen, away from Mrs. Rotolo. "Why didn't she pick a different story?" Lee continued quietly. "Like Noah's Ark. It's not exactly obscure. There's no shortage of merchandise, I bet."

"Lee," Rachel asked, "what's wrong?" Rachel had barely spoken to her friend in over a year. Lee had been too busy, Rachel always assumed, with Paul and their house and their child.

"Do you still love him?" she whispered.

Amazed, Rachel put an arm around her friend. A great deal of heat radiated through the fabric of Lee's shirt. "We were little kids together," Rachel said, trying to calm her. "I love him like that. Just like I love Amy.

Like I love you. Less even. That other business, it was nothing."

"It wasn't nothing," Lee contradicted her. "Paul, he always compares me to you. The whole time I've known him, you've been all he can talk about. Paul, the pastor, Paul's parents, everyone still wishes I was you. They always have."

"No, Lee." Rachel remembered what Amy had said. "You belong, too. You really do."

"Watch them," Lee said. "See if you still believe that."

And Rachel watched, though she already suspected Lee was right. She watched as Paul's father called Rachel by her name while calling Lee, "the daughter-in-law." She watched as Paul's mother grimaced every time Lee spoke; as the pastor and his wife doted on Lee's daughter while ignoring Lee, as though Justine had hatched anonymously from an egg. They didn't even smile when, in the pastor's backyard just before dinner, Lee's daughter held up a cloth puppy and asked Lee to tell the story of its life, which Lee did, entertainingly, patiently.

"Now tell me the story of my life, Mommy," Justine ordered afterward.

"Not now," Lee said kindly. "Mommy needs to take a break right now."

"You don't want to start doing that," Rachel felt compelled to add. She looked at Paul, hard. "If you start telling the story of your life now, you won't ever be able to stop. You'll always do it, even when it hurts other people to hear."

Lee stared at Rachel. It wasn't enough. In the yard next door, a bug-killing lamp sizzled and popped.

"Well, I know the story of my life," Alan said, his voice overly loud. "Blessed and redeemed. That's my story."

"Amen," agreed Paul's mother. And Rachel watched this, just as she watched Paul standing idly by, as oblivious as he'd been, she remembered, at his own wedding, when his mother kept insisting on photographing Paul and Rachel together, under the pretext of nostalgia.

The Rotolos arrived while they all sat eating in the summer evening sunshine at the backyard table. They found seats at the table but declined all offers of food. "You eat," Mr. Rotolo told the pastor's wife. "I can barely even look at food today."

Then, before the plates had even been cleared, Mrs. Rotolo addressed the group. "She told us she's never coming back," she said. "All those years we waited, and now, just when we finally think we can count on her to come around, she's gone again."

"But did she say why?" Lee asked.

"Amy?" Mrs. Rotolo said. "I don't even want to say." She paused. "It's unsavory."

"Drugs?" Paul's mother asked gently.

"Worse," said Mr. Rotolo.

"She's got herself a girlfriend," Mrs. Rotolo admitted. "A lesbian girlfriend."

Paul's mother and Pastor Lou's wife took deep, audible breaths, but Lee, shaking her head, said, "And?"

"And what?" said Mrs. Rotolo.

Lee looked at her. "Is that all?"

"Is that all?" Mrs. Rotolo repeated, her voice rising. "She's a lesbian."

"Amy?" Rachel asked, stunned. "Are you sure?"

"She isn't *really* a lesbian," said Amy's father. "It's just to spite us."

And Rachel understood, finally, the reason for Amy's previous departures. "I can't believe she never told me," she said.

"She never told you because it's not real," Mr. Rotolo argued.

"It's spite," his wife repeated to the group.

"But, wait," Lee interjected, "I don't get it. Why would that make her decide to never come back?"

For a moment, no one said anything. Paul's mother

gave Rachel a reproachful look, similar to one her own mother had given her at her tenth birthday party when a friend from school had given her a Ouija board as a present. It was a look that clearly said, *This person is not one of us. Why is she here? Why aren't you protecting me?*

"It wasn't Amy's choice," Rachel answered Lee at last.

"What?"

"Think about it, Lee. She runs away in high school, then in college. She sets her home up on the other side of the country where no one knows anyone from here. She doesn't tell anyone. Not even *me.* She keeps it secret from anyone who anyone who might tell *them.* Then she waited a bunch of years after she started visiting again, and finally, she decided…she hoped…" Facing Mrs. Rotolo, she continued, "She knew what you'd do if you knew, but she hoped she was wrong and told you anyhow."

"No," answered Mrs. Rotolo.

"And you kicked her out!"

"No," Mrs. Rotolo said again.

"No?" Rachel challenged. "That's exactly what happened."

"No, we gave her an ultimatum."

Rachel gave Pastor Lou a beseeching look.

"The Word does make it very clear," Alan said. "Doesn't it, Pastor? Think of Sodom and Gomorrah. Think of the book of Revelation. Remember who gets cast into the lake of fire?" He counted the damned groups on his fingers as he listed them. "The fearful, the unbelieving, the abominable, the whoremongers, the sorcerers, the idolaters, and the liars."

"You forgot the murderers," Lee said.

"And the murderers," Alan added happily.

"But it doesn't say the lesbians," Rachel said.

"It says the abominable!" Alan shook his head, obviously offended. "Think of Leviticus! The Lord clearly says that homosexuals are an abomination and should be put to death."

"Men," Lee said. "It talks about men. And it also says that eating pork is an abomination."

"Lee," Paul whispered.

Meanwhile, Rachel looked at Alan. "And the New Testament says to love," she said.

Alan looked down, his cheeks flushed.

"You've known Amy her whole life, Pastor," Rachel said.

"Amy has free will," Pastor Lou said.

"And so do we," Rachel went on. "We can choose to love her. And people who can't do *that* can choose to forgive her. Right?"

"Not without repentance," Mrs. Rotolo countered. "You can't have forgiveness without repentance. And Amy's not repenting. She told us. For years, she and this woman, this Theresa, they've been renting a house together, sleeping in the same *bed.* Then she comes to visit *us,* sitting on *our* chairs, eating off *our* forks, sleeping on *our* sheets, and then she goes back to this… this heresy of a marriage… this… this travesty."

"Repent for what?" Lee said. "It's in nature. Even chimpanzees…"

"We are not chimpanzees!" It was Paul's mother who hollered now. "Don't you dare tell my granddaughter that we're chimpanzees."

"Justine?" Lee asked, looking around as though her child had been sitting beside her. "I didn't tell Justine…"

"Unequally yoked," Paul's mother said. "I warned you about this, Paul."

"It's a sin to kick her out of your lives, too!" Rachel interrupted, standing.

"We did not kick her out," Mrs. Rotolo said, standing too. "We gave her a choice. Theresa or us. And don't start with me, Rachel. You wouldn't have made this kind of choice. Don't pretend for a minute that you would have done this to *your* mother."

"You worry about what?" Paul asked his mother.

"She worries about Lee," Rachel said, very quietly. "They only want us to love who *they* choose."

"You're being unfair, Rachel," Paul's mother said. "I understand marrying Alan. I do. But your mother and I made a promise."

"Those promises don't matter anymore," Rachel said. "They never should have mattered." And that's when her vision narrowed until she saw only Amy. "You think you knew my mom?" Rachel heard herself say. "You think you know what she'd forgive? What if I told you that, when me and Paul were teenagers, we had sex, and I got pregnant, and I got an abortion. What if I told you that *my* mom forgave *me*?"

The silence rang momentarily before Paul's father spoke, his mouth a rigid white line. "Did you know this, Paulie?"

Paul looked at Rachel, his eyes half-closed. The simplest required movements: keeping his eyes open, shaking his head, saying no, looked to be beyond his ability. He gazed at his hands the way he had, as a child, whenever Rachel saw him being scolded by his parents or by the pastor. She watched him work his thumb against his cuticles.

"Of course he knew," Rachel persisted. "But he knew what would happen if he told you. The same thing you're all doing to Amy is what you'd've done to him."

"No," Paul said, finally. He opened and closed his mouth many times, but he looked unable to make himself say anything more.

Then his mother asked, "You killed *my* grandchild?"

"No," Paul said again. "It's not true."

"Look at me," said Rachel. "Look at me and tell me that you know for absolute certain it isn't true."

He met her eyes. "But," he said.

And soon, Paul's mother was hugging Lee, rocking her back and forth so hard it seemed they'd both tip over. "I'm sorry," Paul's mother said. "Forgive me, please, Honey. Please forgive me."

"It's no big deal," Lee said back, her voice even. "You don't have anything to apologize for, really."

And, in that moment, perhaps Rachel believed she had fixed Lee's problem as well as Amy's. By contriving an abortion, perhaps she had made herself less deserving of everyone's love than either Lee or Amy. Perhaps now, Paul would be regarded as fortunate to have gotten any wife at all compared to her. Perhaps the Rotolos would count themselves blessed to have Amy as their daughter.

But Mrs. Rotolo didn't express that view. "You kids," she said instead. "What's wrong with all you kids? We trained you up in the way you should go. What happened to all of you?"

"It's a spirit of rebellion," Alan offered. "That's what the Lord's telling me."

"Shut up, Alan!" Lee said.

"Don't," pleaded Rachel.

"Let's all take a breath," said the pastor's wife.

"Lee." Pastor Lou stood. "Why don't you take the baby inside and lie down in the study awhile. You should rest and pray before you go home. Everyone else can clean up. Rachel and Paul, you stay here."

Everyone moved, relieved, it seemed, to be told what to do. Rachel saw Paul trying to catch Lee's eye, but Lee was looking at Rachel.

"Did that make it right?" Rachel asked.

"It's monstrous," Lee answered.

Soon only Rachel, Paul, and the pastor remained in the backyard. Rachel felt a strange collapse of time and remembered a different conversation the three of them had shared, ten years before. They'd all been at the park for a church picnic. It was a summer Sunday, and Rachel and Paul had gone for a walk in the woods. Pastor Lou had surprised them as they stood kissing in a clearing and said, "You know that you're supposed to avoid even the near appearance of evil, don't you? You should be with everyone else, not out here getting hot and heavy."

"We're not getting hot and heavy, Pastor," Rachel had said while Paul stood next to her, staring at his hands.

"You're not playing patty cake," the pastor had answered. But he'd smiled then and had merely threatened to tell their mothers if he ever again caught them similarly engaged. Now, though, he didn't smile. He looked at them as though they were strangers, then down at his feet. "This is very grave," he finally said. "You know that, don't you?"

"It isn't true," Paul insisted, with those same lowered, fearful eyes. Rachel remembered him as a child, shirtless with a pudgy belly and pale nipples, as they played in a small, plastic pool in this very backyard. She remembered the first time she kissed him, his tongue large and wet against hers, and, three years later, the ecstasy of feeling his hands on her breasts. He knew her more fully than anyone, even Alan, and yet, she saw, he didn't know whether this was true.

"He doesn't want to admit it," she said.

"You won't repent, Paul?"

"It didn't happen," he answered.

"You didn't have intercourse?"

He shook his head. Rachel's memory of him as a child wouldn't leave. She used to stand in that plastic kiddie pool and splash him mercilessly, and his father would angrily tell him to "man up" when he cried about the water in his eyes and ears. "We were careful," Paul told Pastor Lou. "She was on the Pill."

"I lied," Rachel said. "I lied." She remembered again how it had felt to kiss him, and how everything in her had quickened with the feelings of discovery you can have only once.

"You should have gotten married," the pastor was saying. "The church would have been able to support you in that. We can't support you here. It's murder."

"There's forgiveness for murderers," Rachel said.

"That's not what Alan says it says in Revelations," Paul reminded her.

"Revelation," Rachel corrected. "There's no s."

"You sound like Lee." He finally raised his head and looked at her. Then he blinked and regarded the pastor. "Saul was a murderer before he was redeemed," he said.

"When Saul was struck down on the road to Damascus, he was not a Christian. After he repented and became Paul, he was different. He didn't sin after that. He couldn't have. Not with the living word of Christ in his heart." He stroked his chin. Rachel hadn't before noticed how much Pastor Lou looked like an old man. She hadn't noticed that he no longer had a vigorous, sinewy body capable of near gymnastic displays of energy at the pulpit. He no longer had thick black hair or smooth olive skin. Beneath his silver hair, everything about him had grown slack and fragile. He was older than her parents, she reminded herself. He had to be older than sixty.

"Rachel," he said. "You'll need to get cleansed of the spirits you've been carrying before I'll let you back in the church. Alan can still come in the meanwhile, naturally, but you'll have to meet with me for marriage counseling once you've gotten right with God." A worry seemed to possess him and he asked, "Did your mother get right with God before she died?"

"Yes," Rachel answered. "My mother was always right with God."

Pastor Lou stood. "I need to go inside to minister to Lee," he said. "Rachel, you should go home."

Rachel nodded. She left through the side gate because it seemed obedient to avoid leaving through the house. She stood at the perimeter of the yard, watching Paul pick up the evening's remaining plates and cups. Years and years ago, she remembered, they had snuck off in her father's big blue Chevy. They'd found a dead end street that led to a little path in the woods, and that's where they would park, in the front seat, sitting up, their clothes mostly on. One night, their last summer together, they'd fought in the car immediately afterward. Facing Paul, her knees against his hips, she felt their bodies unlock as they argued. What had they fought about? Rachel was leaving for college and had begged him to come with her. But he couldn't. Just the thought of broaching the topic with his parents seemed to have paralyzed him with fear. "It's bad enough we do *this*," he said. "We never should have done this without being married."

"You don't want to?" Rachel asked.

"It's not that," Paul said. "It's just... it would kill them if they knew, and it was *your* idea."

"*My* idea?" Rachel said. Their fingers were still interlaced, and she felt her grip tighten.

"And now you want me to do something worse!" Paul continued.

"Moving away with me is *worse*?" Rachel asked. "Worse than what, Paul? Worse than making love to me?"

He looked away. "I don't know," he said. "I guess maybe."

And, overcome with rage, Rachel had bent Paul's fingers back until one popped.

After Rachel left for school, they argued over the phone for months, but that night on the dead end street, she supposed, was when they'd truly begun to split up.

Rachel watched Paul pile the plates and cups he'd gathered on the pastor's backyard table. Afterward, he sat, doing nothing. The night grew darker. Nearby houses brightened or darkened from within, and fireflies peppered the air with their teasing light. She thought, again, of how she, Paul, and Amy chased them during those long ago summertime prayer meetings, back when people still brought tambourines. How cheerful salvation had sounded back then, clean and easy and full of light.

Finally, Pastor Lou came out into the yard again and Rachel started walking home. The pastor had already told her to leave. She didn't think to question or to disobey him, just as she didn't question or disobey him the next morning when he phoned to tell her about Damascus House.

***

Now, as she struggled to get comfortable in the scratchy sheets Damascus House provided, she missed the warm bulk of Alan's body beside hers, his hand clasped around her wrist, a compromise they'd made long ago, because Rachel wanted to fall asleep in Alan's arms, but Alan couldn't fall asleep except on his own side of the bed, lying on his back.

"If you don't succeed here," Father Frank had said, "your husband and your church will not be willing to take you back."

She needed Alan to take her back. She only had five thousand dollars of her own, she reminded herself. Where could she go? She remembered the in-ground pool Amy's parents had once had. Whenever summertime prayer meetings happened in the Rotolos' backyard, the adults would pray while she, Amy, and Paul dove into the deep end and raced to the bottom. It was quiet under the water. A few summers ago, the Rotolos had gotten the pool drained. It was too much trouble, they'd said. Now, she missed the water's hush. She wanted to find Amy deep in the water, the way they had as children, their wet hands interlocking as they surfaced.

Five thousand dollars would get her to Oregon, she realized. If Alan didn't take her back, five thousand dollars would be more than enough to get to Amy's. It was rebellion, she knew. But rebellion, she finally decided, wasn't always a sin. Sometimes, as it was for Amy, rebellion was a necessity. Or maybe it wasn't even rebellion? Maybe, at some point, what constitutes rebellion in childhood simply becomes making an adult's choices? All day, Rachel had referenced her age in protest, and yet, like a child, she'd obeyed the house's rules and schedule, had eaten their meals, and had even agreed to sleep alone in the stupid, teen-sized bed of this monastic little cell.

She found herself standing, pulling on her yellow jumpsuit, and making her way into the hall.

The Damascus House common areas were completely deserted. She worried, fleetingly, where the staff slept. Surely they didn't live on-site in little dormitory rooms. On the ground floor, she contemplated looking for her purse but decided against it. She would call Alan or the pastor. "This is a children's ministry," she would say, and they would, perhaps, bring her home. If they wouldn't, she could call Amy. She wouldn't have to do anything more.

She worried again at the front door, looked for cameras, and braced herself. Maybe, she thought, an alarm system would play that horrible hymn? But the door unlocked easily and opened silently. She was running across the lawn. She was free.

But she wasn't free, of course. Someone stood at the gates separating the property from the outside world, shining a flashlight in her path. Its beam found her eyes; purple splotches remained, obscuring her vision. A moment later, she smelled perfume and felt Grace's hand on her elbow.

"The Lord put you on my heart," she said.

"I can't be here," she told Grace. "It isn't right."

"I'm sure it feels that way," Grace purred. "But this is what God wants us to do. He wants us to discipline each other, like He disciplines us."

"No," Rachel said. And now her escape seemed childish, too. How could she have decided to run off, without money or identification, in her crazy yellow jumpsuit? Tomorrow morning, she would tell Father Frank and his wife that she had decided to leave. She would collect her purse and earrings. Then, in her street clothes and in the daylight, she'd exit through the front door.

I am twenty-six years old, she told herself, and this time her age sounded right.

"I'll leave in the morning," Rachel said. "Please let go of me."

And Grace obeyed.

Purge

Linda Rotolo stood ironing her husband's shirts in the spare bedroom. Now that Vic was older, his shirts never laundered clean, and Linda could smell his acrid sweat in the iron's steam. When she finished, she would hang the shirts in Amy's bedroom closet. Then she would clear Amy's room of everything her daughter had left behind.

Amy was gone again. This time, Linda knew, she was gone for good.

Just a handful of mornings ago, they'd all sat together at the kitchen table—poor Vic still wore his pajamas and looked half-asleep—and Amy had said, "I need to tell you about Theresa."

From her wallet, Amy had extracted a photograph of an Italian woman with long black hair. Linda was so busy looking at the picture that she almost didn't hear her daughter say, "We've been lovers for five years." The words made no sense. Lovers, Linda thought. What did that mean?

"I've lied to you my whole life," Amy had said. "But Theresa saved me from that."

Linda set the iron down; the hot water splashed and sizzled. Amy's use of the word "saved" bothered her most.

Amy had run away twice before, as a teenager and as a young adult, and, both times, Linda thought she'd die of shame. Her friends from church had fasted and prayed, but no one could understand what she'd done. Not this time. This time, everything added up. At the prayer meeting the night after Amy left, Rachel had defended Amy, but on the telephone just yesterday, Kathleen, the pastor's wife, had said, "You did the right thing."

"It wasn't that I wanted to kick her out of our lives," Linda said.

"Of course not," said Kathleen.

"If it were just this one thing," Linda explained. "If this were the only thing she'd ever done."

"It's the final straw," the pastor's wife agreed.

"And now Rachel's gone, too."

"Don't," Kathleen replied. "There's still hope there."

From her place at the ironing board, Linda could see into the house next door, where Paul and Lee, one of the church's younger married couples, lived. Linda had never before cared for Lee. She'd been an interloper of sorts, an oddity from outside Riverview, a newcomer to the church. Paul had been pledged to Rachel from his earliest days, and over the years, Rachel had sometimes felt like a daughter to Linda, the daughter Linda often wished she could have had. True, Rachel didn't have Amy's talent or charm, but Linda had always mistakenly believed in Rachel's goodness, her purity of spirit. But, a few days ago, she'd confessed to having aborted a child, Paul's child, as a teenager. She had even falsely claimed that her mother had known and forgiven her, even though Linda, who'd been Rachel's mother's best friend, knew Susan would never have forgiven such a thing. Now, Rachel was at an out of state ministry the pastor had found, and next door, Paul and Lee fought late at night, their voices carrying.

Everyone had wanted Paul and Rachel to marry. When Rachel chose Alan instead, Linda had blamed Paul, believing Rachel had chosen Alan because his faith was so much stronger. Like everyone else at church in the early 90s, Linda suspected the eve of the apocalypse had arrived, and Alan, a true disciple, seemed a better choice than passive, lukewarm Paul. But now, she regretted having wished Rachel for either man. Now, she thought both Amy and Rachel deserved to be alone.

More than twenty years ago, when Linda had first joined the church, when she'd first met Rachel's mother, Susan, they'd both been so proud of their darling, pink babies. They were young mothers, only twenty-one years old; each had gotten married at age eighteen, and by the time the babies were born, each had decided that marriage was, well, not at all what they'd once had in mind. Neither of them had been to college. Neither of them had ever pursued a career. They only had their daughters, the church, one another, and soon, the other young mothers from the congregation with whom they met for luncheons and prayer meetings and Bible studies. They brought their babies and their tambourines; they wore their hair long.

Amy and Rachel were such pretty little girls, both of them; they both had black hair, gray eyes, and Italian chins. But that resemblance grew less pronounced as the girls grew, the way a resemblance between siblings sometimes can. And how different they became, too! They stayed loyal to one another, of course, but until a few days ago, it seemed Rachel had grown ever sweeter while Amy had grown more and more rebellious.

Linda and Susan had once pitied Kathleen, the pastor's wife, who was older than the other women from church. Kathleen had lost two babies some years before they'd all met and had nearly run out of hope. The other women had prayed for Kathleen, their hands on her shoulders. But she'd never gotten pregnant again. These days, Linda envied her.

"What did we do wrong?" Vic had asked that final morning, looking at the snapshot of Theresa as though it would speak to him.

"Nothing," Amy had answered. "It's just who I am."

But Linda didn't believe her. She wasn't *really* a lesbian, Linda and Vic agreed silently across the table. She simply knew that *acting* like one would help her achieve her desired end. When she'd run away the previous time, as a young adult, her guilt had likely been too strong. She'd run away for no reason at all. She wouldn't have been able to justify it. So she'd come back. This time, she'd probably wanted to make her departure stick, to have a clear-cut story she could tell, so she made this, this *lifestyle choice* that was wholly irreconcilable with Linda and Vic's values, and, what's more, with the Lord's values. What could Linda do? She gave Amy an ultimatum, and Amy chose Theresa. Amy had probably gone home to that woman, acting the victim, pretending her parents had cast her out, pretending she hadn't run away at all.

"We must have done something," Vic persisted.

It wasn't as though they hadn't made any mistakes. Of course they'd made mistakes. But other parents did worse; other parents barely noticed their children and didn't trouble themselves to feel guilty about it, or they neglected or abused them, were selfish or preoccupied, or blamed their children for their own failings. From Amy, they had merely expected results.

Linda often bristled when others colloquially misquoted Proverbs 22:6 as "Raise up a child in the way he should go and when he is old, he will not depart from it." The scripture did not say "raise." It said "train." And Linda had invested an awful lot in Amy's training, material and spiritual. No child had ever been given the kinds of opportunities Amy had enjoyed. And no parent, Linda believed, had ever received so poor a return on her investments.

Many years ago, before Vic learned to work the market and got rich, during months when they could barely pay their mortgage, they'd paid for Amy's lessons in singing, piano, clarinet, dance, gymnastics, guitar, ice skating. And, yes, Linda had hoped, given myriad training, Amy would be exceptional at *something*. But Amy became just good enough at everything to get the attention of those more mediocre than she. Worse yet, they had to force her to keep up her end of things. They shamed her into practicing for her music lessons. They compelled her to stick to her diets so she wouldn't grow too fat for dancing or gymnastics.

How many times, during Amy's high school years, had Linda hung a weight chart on the refrigerator because Amy, once again, grew heavier than 120 pounds?

If she'd been a stupid or untalented child, Linda wouldn't have set the bar as high. But she'd shown so much promise. When Amy was still a baby, Linda had posted signs on everything they'd owned: STOVE, REFRIGERATOR, COUCH. And she'd worked with Amy, teaching her reading and phonics skills. Because of Linda, Amy could read by the time she was three years old. But school interfered, first transforming Amy merely into a high achiever, then later, into a paragon of mediocrity, an overweight girl more interested in figuring out how to use hairspray on her bangs than in excelling at anything.

Linda should have sent Amy to a Christian high school, or at the very least, a Christian college. She shouldn't have been so quick to send Amy to the best school that would take her. Linda had danced around the living room when Amy's acceptance letter from a small, private girls' university came in the mail. Even though Amy's lackluster grade point average had disqualified her from the most prestigious schools, Linda and Vic had paid extravagantly for Amy to attend SAT preparatory classes, and consequently, her test scores were high enough for second tier schools to offer her entrance. Amy's school cost more than twenty thousand dollars a year, and they paid it. The Christmas of her freshman year, Amy could only boast a C average and a personal high weight of 124 pounds. 124 pounds! At 5'4"! Linda, herself, never allowed her own weight to exceed 105 pounds, even though she and Amy stood less than half and inch apart! Then, just before Easter, Amy dropped out, sending home a letter—a letter!—explaining she'd chosen to work awhile instead of going to college and wouldn't be coming home. It was too late in the semester for Vic and Linda to receive a refund on any of the tuition they'd paid.

Linda had been happily anticipating Amy's arrival at Easter, hoping her daughter would bring home better grades than she had the previous term or some morsel of good news: a lead in the college musical, perhaps, or a solo in the choir. The college had a gymnastics team, but Amy hadn't bothered trying out for it, even though gymnastics would have been her best chance for a scholarship. Amy had competed in gymnastics since the age of nine, and although she'd never won individual metals in state or even county-wide meets, she'd often contributed scores that helped her teams win group honors. Plus, she was the one who'd braid the other girls' hair, tape their hurt ankles, and decorate their lockers with "break a leg" balloons. The girls would telephone Amy with their problems. Once, Linda overheard Amy on the phone, saying, genuinely, "That's wonderful!" to a teammate whose parents had reconciled though they'd been on the seeming verge of divorce. This from a girl who couldn't seem to care less when it came to her own family, her own parents who'd sacrificed endlessly for her, who'd gone without new clothes for years on end so Amy could wear clothes fit for a princess. "That's wonderful," she'd said to some gymnastics friend. Linda could have strangled her.

But instead of spending a happy holiday dinner with her daughter, Linda prayed with her friends from church. Poor little Rachel, home from Christian college, had rested her head on Linda's knees, assuring, "She didn't call me. I don't know where she is."

After Amy dropped out of college, Linda didn't hear from her for three years. Finally, after hiring a private investigator to track down her own child, Linda steeled her courage and wrote Amy a letter; then she flew to Portland, Oregon, the city nearest to the town where Amy had decided to move. Amy consented to the meeting, giving Linda an hour—an hour!—of time in Linda's Portland hotel room. Amy had said she would meet Linda but would not allow her to "show up" in her town, at her home, or at her workplace. Show up! As if Linda were a dangerous stranger! Amy didn't know, of course, probably couldn't even have imagined, what it was like for Linda to fly there. Never before had Linda flown on a plane alone, stayed in a hotel alone, or even eaten in a restaurant alone. But, there she was, flying alone from New Jersey to Oregon, taking, alone, the long, overpriced taxi ride from the Portland Airport to her hotel. The cab driver, a self-confessed Christian, prayed with her in the cab but overcharged her anyway. She paid the fare without complaining but it wasn't that she hadn't noticed. The love of money was the root of all evil, and Christians, Linda knew, weren't exempt. How many pyramid schemes had other members of the church tried to ensnare her and Vic in over the years? How many times had other members of their own church, even their closest friends, jealous of the prosperity Vic had attained, speculated loudly about his supposed Mafia connections? Linda agreed with the criticism that it was Christians who gave Christians a bad name. But, because they were Christians, they would all be forgiven, whereas Amy, well, she had rejected her forgiveness.

At the hotel, a twenty-one year old Amy explained that she'd suffered at her mother's hands. Yes, suffered.

Amy gave an example: one day, in kindergarten, coming home with a less-than-perfect seatwork assignment, she'd been confident that her mother wouldn't be angry. But Linda *had* been angry. She'd expected Amy's work to be perfect. Listening to Amy talk, her head lowered so dramatically, Linda couldn't remember the incident at all. She only remembered later years when Amy had brought home Bs and Cs and Linda had been more than understanding, believing Amy's half-baked excuses about vengeful, ineffective teachers, believing that Amy, who barely did any homework at all, had "tried hard" as she'd claimed. What bullshit. Had she pressured Amy too much in those early years of school? Maybe. Probably. But so what? Poor Rachel had spent years watching her mother cry while her father drank and watched TV. Linda herself had seen things as a child she'd never talk about to anyone. And Amy cried trauma over Linda's reaction to a kindergarten assignment? Linda flew home from Portland, fully expecting never to hear from Amy again.

Then, not long after, the Gulf War happened, and Amy called to ask if she could visit from time to time. Linda attributed this change of heart to the war; Amy had been trained to know the prophecies, after all. They paid for Amy's airline tickets, of course, and brought her to church with them, but although Amy lowered her head and closed her eyes during the prayers, she never spoke aloud nor raised her hands in praise and worship. She didn't belong to a church at home, she told them, as though desperate to hurt Linda with this information.

When Amy had first dropped out of college and had sent that awful letter, Linda was unable to stop remembering the young prostitutes in the Bronx who'd worked on the block where she'd grown up. How beautiful they were, in a way, moving through the dusk on their long, spidery legs and noisy shoes. As a child, she'd often stared at their strange, pained gaits, heavily painted eyes, and brazen despair. Linda was sure Amy had joined them and that theirs was, in some way, the unavoidable fate of girls who disappeared from their homes. She believed Amy would come back, small and spindly as an umbrella, her eyes penitent. Humbled and broken, she'd lie in the bed she'd had since childhood and Linda would somehow find it possible to forgive her, to pray for her, and Amy would rebound, filled with the Lord's love and unwilling to sin or to leave again.

But that isn't what happened. Amy had come back to visit, it was true, but she'd come back even bigger in some ways than she'd been when she'd left. She wasn't fat anymore but she certainly wasn't small. Her arms and shoulders rippled with muscles, and, oddly, she'd grown at least two inches since she'd last lived at home. Her long hair, which, in high school, she had teased and sprayed and tortured, was prematurely gray and fell in simple waves. Often, she pulled it back into a ponytail. She didn't wear any make-up. And she certainly didn't have the humble, downcast eyes of a prodigal. She'd put herself through nursing school, she bragged, and she lived and worked in small town Oregon where, after her shifts at the hospital, she played on a nurses' volleyball team and took art classes for fun at the local college. She bragged about her volleyball serve. She bragged about learning to blow glass.

Amy said she loved Oregon. The whole state felt like a personal affront to Linda, who knew Amy had chosen Oregon simply because it was as far from New Jersey as she could possibly get. But Amy claimed her town was beautiful. Cheap, she said, and full of gardens. You can ride your bike from anywhere to anywhere, she said, and you never have to get off the bike path. In the summers, she said, the sun stayed out past nine and the whole town bloomed with blackberries. She bragged about baking blackberry pies from scratch.

"I don't want to hear about your stupid town!" Linda had finally shouted. Probably nothing Amy said about it was true. Probably it was strip malls and parking lots, like everywhere else.

And Amy *was* a liar. She had told lies from nearly the moment she knew how to speak—little lies, kids' lies at first; at three years old, for example, she'd walked around the pastor's living room telling everyone she had blonde hair. By age six, strange behaviors got added to the lies; she began wearing a knit cap every day, summer and winter, for a year. Her hair started falling out. She only dispensed with the cap one afternoon when she pulled her shirt over her head while getting ready for a bath and the shirt's collar caught on her hat, knocking it into the toilet. The toilet was clean, of course, but to Amy, the hat must never have seemed the same. After she gave up the hat, she began to bite the insides of her mouth until they bled, and in the mornings, Linda would find Amy's pillowcase stained with dried blood. After many punishments, that habit stopped and Amy bit her arms instead, giving herself so many purple bruises that Linda feared she'd be suspected of child abuse. Sometimes, too, Amy went to bed in her pajamas then surreptitiously changed into her school clothes. Linda and Vic would stand at her bedside, the overhead light on, demanding she change back into something appropriate. Later every night, poor Vic would sneak into her room after she was asleep, pulling back the covers to make sure she hadn't changed clothes again.

Meanwhile, year by year, her lies intensified. She'd come home from school announcing the most preposterous things. She was so much smarter than the rest of her kindergarten class, she said at age five, that she'd been put in her own reading group. Linda called the teacher, delighted. Amy was doing fine, the teacher said. But the special reading group didn't exist. At age eight, when Amy fell off the school jungle gym, cracking her head open so that it required stitches, she blamed her fall on a girl in her class. Linda had sat with Amy at the kitchen table, holding a toy baton the way one would hold a monkey bar. "Show me," she told her daughter. "Show me how she pushed you." But as Amy grappled with Linda's grip in different ways, it became evident she'd fallen of her own accord. Again and again, Linda reminded the Lord of His promise: "Train up a child in the way she should go, and when she is old, she will not depart from it." She consulted Susan, the pastor, and her Bible. She spent hours in prayer with the other women from the church. And, most of all, she gave her daughter more, much more, than she gave her husband or herself.

Linda finished ironing Vic's shirts and started on his trousers. She wished she understood the source of Amy's evil spirits. The pastor had been praying with Linda and Susan at Linda's house the first time he identified them. Amy, as usual, had done something terrible. It could have been any number of things. Perhaps it was the time she told her gymnastics team that her father was Jewish and had grown up in Alaska, the time she told her classmates that she was adopted, the time she was caught shoplifting at Sears, or the time she hid a pack of cigarettes in her desk drawer.

Whatever the incident, abruptly, mid-prayer, the pastor led Linda into her daughter's uncannily tidy bedroom. At school, Amy's locker always smelled of something festering, but Amy's bedroom, year by year, remained neat as a museum. Her clothes were folded impeccably in her dresser. Her bed was made without wrinkles. The room was so clean and still that you could smell the subtly spicy wood of the cedar chest below the window. A cup of pencils sat on her desktop. The pastor looked around, and upon opening the desk's bottom drawer, emptied what looked to be reams of used notebook paper.

The pastor, Susan, and Linda all sat on the carpet, their knees touching, and rifled through the pages.

On each, Amy had drawn faces, women's faces, with shell-shocked eyes. Some of the pictures bore the same inscrutable caption: "All snowflakes alike." As they dug through the pile, Linda felt newly terrified of her daughter. Amy had loved to draw and color as a little child, but she'd never been properly trained—Linda had never, for example, enrolled Amy in art classes. She couldn't fathom why she would spend so much time drawing these awful pictures when there was music to practice and homework to do.

"I don't understand," Linda had said.

"It's demons," the pastor had explained, "evil spirits." And although it sounded strange to Linda, even ludicrous, together they'd cast out the spirits, laying hands on the desk, and carting those disgusting pictures away in plastic bags. Afterward, the room's atmosphere *did* feel an awful lot lighter. Even Susan agreed, saying, "It feels like a whole new room."

In church that following Sunday, Pastor Lou announced to the congregation that he'd met a young man on the Boardwalk with a calling to discern spirits, and, by praying with him, the Lord had anointed the pastor to discern spirits, too. He called Alan to the front of the church, but Linda hadn't paid any attention to Alan then. She only looked at the pastor; his face glowed as though it reflected the grace of God itself. *This is what an archangel looks like*, Linda thought as Pastor Lou addressed the congregation's teenagers—only sixty or seventy of them back in those days, a gangly crew of attitudes and angles—scattered throughout the rows, some seated in little cliques. He said that Alan could serve as a model for them, that they had all grown complacent in their salvation, that they all took it for granted. He told them to come kneel at the altar, and they obeyed.

"To you who have been given much, much is expected," the pastor said as he laid his hands on the kids' heads one by one. Linda, Susan, and Paul's mother joyfully clasped one another. And Linda thought of the possessed man in the gospels whose demons, when cast out by Christ, were legion enough to fill a herd of swine. The world was even darker now, even more full of sin and danger, and kids like Amy were susceptible every moment. Their salvation was their only safeguard, but they'd gotten saved so easily, so effortlessly, and so long ago, that they had no idea what salvation cost nor how to maintain it. Without their parents' vigilance, kids like Amy would succumb to a multitude of temptations. At the altar, Paul and Rachel lay slain in the spirit, but Amy just knelt there, her head level. Afterward, Rachel ran down the aisle and into Susan's arms and Paul kissed his mother's cheek. But Amy only stared at Linda with strangely hooded eyes, a defiant expression Linda had never seen her possess before, though, after that day, it never went away.

In the car on the way home from church, when Linda said, "The Lord really worked something beautiful in Rachel and Paul today," Amy scoffed and looked out the window.

"She's going to murder us," Vic said that night. "One night, she'll kill us in our sleep." It was true, Linda thought now. In a way, Amy had done exactly that.

The last time Amy ran away, Linda stopped eating. For months, Vic stopped working. They could have lost the house, it got so bad. Thank God for Susan and the Bianchis. Thank God for the church. Thank God for Rachel, who called Linda every day for months, and who visited every time she came home from college.

But, a year or so after Amy's disappearance, Rachel and Amy must have started talking again. Rachel denied it, but Linda could tell. She remained thoughtful toward Linda. She still telephoned on Linda's birthday and on Mother's Day, but something had shifted. Linda begged her for information: where Amy was, why she had left, if she was all right, but

Rachel always lied, "I don't know, Mrs. Rotolo. I'm sorry." At the time, Linda couldn't fathom it. Rachel was such a good girl, Linda thought. How could she agree to keep Amy's secrets? But she didn't know, then, what Rachel herself had done. She didn't know the war had already been lost. Probably, Rachel had also confided in Amy. Probably, Amy had agreed to keep Rachel's secret, too.

Linda stopped ironing and carried an empty box and Vic's clothes into Amy's room. She thought about emptying the desk drawers first but decided not to. Once the desk was empty, Amy would truly be gone. She started with the dresser instead. She dusted the gorgeous ceramic lamp she'd bought from Lionel's Furniture back when Amy was three years old. The lamp had two bulbs, one regular bulb and one nightlight, though Amy had always insisted on keeping her door closed and her room dark. Linda unplugged the lamp and put it in the box. Next, she opened the jewelry box that played "Jesus Loves Me" when its lid was lifted. The box's aging red velvet lining issued a delicate upsurge of dust that sparkled like the trinkets Linda and Vic had bought for their daughter: sweet gold crucifixes on tremulously thin gold chains, three pairs of diamond earrings, thick gold bracelets, an expensive watch with changeable wristbands Linda had bought for Amy's seventeenth birthday, a high school class ring with a blue stone rather than garnet, Amy's birthstone, because Amy thought her birthstone was "ugly. Like blood." She packed the jewelry box next to the lamp.

As a child and teenager, Amy had been gracious enough in accepting multitudes of things, but Linda noticed that almost everything her daughter had received remained in this room. The one thing Amy seemed to have taken was a Holly Hobbie doll that had been a gift, long ago, from Vic's father. It seemed the doll had stayed behind the last time Amy disappeared; Linda remembered its place on the cedar chest between the Raggedy Ann and Andy dolls Susan had hand sewn when Amy was a baby. But this time, the Holly Hobbie doll was gone. Vic's father had ingratiated himself to Amy in recent years, Linda recalled. A couple of years ago, when they'd gone to Vic's parents' house for Christmas, Vic's father had asked Amy to pour him a beer.

"Don't you dare," Linda had warned. But Amy had done it anyway, telling Linda that the man could have a beer if he wanted one. When Amy poured it, though, the old man had laughed, "You don't drink, do you?"

"What? How do you know?"

"Look at my glass," he'd said. "It's all foam! A real

drinker knows how to pour beer." He took the bottle from Amy and demonstrated. "Like that," he'd said, and the liquid rolled, without froth, from the mouth of the bottle.

"Tell that to *her*," Amy practically spat, pointing at Linda.

"I never said you drank," Linda had replied.

But she *had* worried that Amy drank. She had worried about everything except the one thing she ought to have. When Amy said she was learning to blow glass, Linda thought of glass bongs and hash pipes. When Amy talked about her volleyball team, Linda pictured stereotypical after-game beer fests. When she noticed that Amy never once mentioned a man, Linda worried that Amy had too many boyfriends to name, that she was what once would have been called "loose." But it never occurred to her that Amy would have become something even worse than a drinker, a marijuana smoker, an easy girl.

She boxed the Raggedy Ann and Andy dolls and opened the spicy-scented cedar chest. Inside, she found blankets Vic's mother had crocheted before Amy was born, equal parts blue and pink because, in those days, a baby's gender was always a surprise, or white and lumpy, patterned with malformed yellow ducks in crooked rows. Amy had never used them.

She hadn't been the kind of child with an attachment to blankets. For her, it had been that hat.

Beneath the blankets lay Amy's high school yearbook. Linda thumbed through it, reading the clichéd inscriptions by other teenagers. Had Amy been popular? Linda looked through the pages on which those who'd been voted "most likely to succeed" and "prettiest eyes" appeared. Amy wasn't there. But she was pictured with the gymnastics team, the chorus, the stage band, and the drama club. And she belonged to the art club. Linda hadn't known that. She saw Amy posed with the "artistic" high-schoolers—all the girls except Amy had those horrible spiked haircuts that looked like pineapple tops—and understood why Amy had kept that particular club membership secret: the only boy in the photograph was Amy's friend, Tom, a boy who wasn't from the church and to whom Linda had forbidden her to speak after she'd overheard Tom use the phrase "mental masturbation" while he and Amy sat together, talking, in the backyard. "Are you having sex with him?" Linda had demanded after sending Tom home.

"Oh, Mother," Amy had replied. "What do you think?"

She hadn't known what to think, but she'd taken Amy to a Christian doctor who'd verified her daughter's virginity and had given her a drug test to boot. Looking at the yearbook photo, Linda finally understood. One thing only explained a teenage boy in a high school art club. And Amy? No, Linda thought, looking at the photo. Amy looked so feminine with her teased hair. She was gazing up at Tom, her schoolgirl eyes wide. She was in love with Tom, Linda decided.

She set the yearbook aside. Later, she'd tear out all the pages and throw them in the trash compactor.

Linda hung Vic's pressed shirts and pants in Amy's closet. It, too, held nothing significant. Amy's old high school varsity jacket hung in the back, the pins for team captain and all-around competitor attached to the varsity letter. Amy hadn't become captain because of her gymnastics skills; that was certain. But she had always been able to charm her way into getting what she wanted. The pastor had even remarked on that once. "Amy is charming," he'd said. "You should be careful." But Linda hadn't been careful. She'd only wanted to be honored and obeyed by someone of her own flesh and blood. Unfortunately, the mantle fell to Amy.

Linda folded and placed Amy's long ago clothes in the cardboard box; only the desk remained untouched. This desk and its attendant miseries, Linda thought. Aside from those horrible drawings, she had also found notes Amy had written to that awful Tom, notes that made fun of the church or told lies, notes that bore anti-Christian doodles or even bad language. The Bible said that everyone reaps what he or she sows. In prayer, Linda often asked God what in the world she had sown to deserve a daughter like Amy.

The top two desk drawers were empty; dust and old paper clips stuck in the crevices where wood met wood. But Amy had always kept her secrets in the bottom drawer. No matter how many times Linda searched this desk, Amy never changed her hiding place, as though she had wanted her mother to find what she put there. What might it be this time? Wildly, she expected a journal, written in her daughter's hand, explaining everything. No. More likely it would be a single, fat, white envelope with the word "Linda" written on its front and a note inside that read, "This won't make up for anything, but it's all I can give you." Within the note, Linda would find a thick stack of crisp hundred dollar bills—perhaps a hundred of them, ten thousand dollars' worth, half of the tuition they'd wasted on her. And this would be Amy's meager payback. After years of praying and fasting, of forgiving Amy's failings and sins and waiting for her repentance, it would all come down to a scribbled note and ten thousand dollars. She held her breath and opened the drawer.

Nothing.

In the Gospels, Jesus "gave up the ghost" after saying, "Father, forgive them. They know not what they do." The pastor always said it was Jesus' choice to die. He died, the pastor said, of a broken heart. Linda thought she understood that now. She felt as though her body might cleave in two. The room grew dark around her.

Finally, through the window, she saw Lee, Paul's wife, turning lights on in the house next door. Lee, with her shuffling gate and pale face, looked as though she occupied her own home as a stranger. Lee was the kind of girl who'd never been given anything. Not like Amy. Amy, it seemed clear, had always been given far too much. Linda took the box of Amy's old things and carried it next door.

"What is this?" Lee asked, her eyes large in her thin face.

"Keep it," Linda said.

Lee peered inside the box, seeming to notice the baby blankets. "For Justine?" she asked in a flat, small voice.

"It's all for you," she told Lee. "Some of it's valuable. I know you haven't had a lot."

Lee blinked rapidly as though about to be slapped.

"You don't have to give me anything, Mrs. Rotolo." She found the jewelry box beneath the blankets and shook her head. "These are Amy's," she said. "I can't take Amy's stuff."

She could bring this box of gifts to Rachel instead, she thought, once Rachel had returned from the ministry. Rachel would wrap her arms around Linda's neck and say, "I was wrong, Mrs. Rotolo. Amy didn't deserve a mother like you." But Linda knew Rachel wouldn't come home behaving that way. Kathleen Bianchi might believe hope remained, but Linda knew better. Linda understood that, once these kids were lost, nothing brought them back.

The jewelry box and blankets still sat in Lee's hands as Linda began running, hard and fast as a child, back to her own empty house.

Merkava

As the taxi pulled along the curb in front of his house, Alan watched through the living room window and felt his faith flicker. The Bible commanded to pray without ceasing, and for the past three days, he had done that; he had stood in faith for Rachel's repentance. Repentance, Pastor Lou always said, was not a simple matter of apology. The word derived from the Hebrew *shuv*, which meant to turn around. If Rachel had stayed at the ministry for the full month that had been prescribed, Alan was sure God would have shown her what repentance truly meant and she would have come back righteous and rededicated to the Lord. Instead, she'd insisted on leaving the ministry practically the moment she'd arrived. Now, just three days after her departure, a taxi had retrieved her from the airport—Pastor Lou had recommended that Alan not do so—and was delivering her home.

The pastor had also warned Alan that Rachel could be harboring spirits even more intractable than those she'd left with. She could stay home for one night, the pastor said, but Alan and she needed to spend it in prayer. First thing tomorrow morning, he would meet with both of them to discuss next steps. Ministries other than Damascus House existed. She would have to choose one and to pledge compliance.

Rachel got out of the taxi. She approached the house with a suitcase in one hand. It occurred to Alan, as it did regularly, that neither the Apostle Paul nor Jesus Christ had taken a wife and that theirs was the most sensible course of action. *Pray for wisdom*, Alan heard the quiet voice of the Lord admonish in his ear. So he closed his eyes and chastised himself for wishing he'd chosen a different life, one of celibacy and waiting.

He knew he should meet Rachel in the driveway, take her bag, and smile at her in welcome, but he couldn't. His body prickled with the childhood memory of looking through the front window at his father's car as his father arrived home from work. Stop, he told himself. He was blessed with a new father, a heavenly father, whose mercy and goodness knew no end.

Pray for wisdom, Alan heard the Lord remind him, and again Alan repented for his despair.

He opened the door.

"Hi, Alan." Alan tried hopefully to see the

light of Jesus in Rachel's eyes, but their expression communicated nothing.

Misery lodged in his throat. "How was your flight?"

"Fine," she answered. "I'm just tired."

She walked quickly toward their bedroom, shutting the door behind her. He approached and quietly asked, "Why are you back so soon?"

"Not now, Alan."

Pray for wisdom, Alan heard the Lord repeat.

"Praise You, Jesus," Alan began.

"And please don't pray by the door," Rachel called. "Please. I need to sleep."

Give me wisdom, Lord, Alan prayed silently. Guide my steps.

And he distinctly heard the Lord reply, *Go outside and wash the cars.*

He often heard the Lord make unfathomable requests like this, and although he always chose to obey, Alan understood that others would probably consider him crazy, or at the very least, ridiculous. He was the only Born-again Christian at the office supply company where he spent his days entering sales numbers and orders into databases (sometimes, to cheer himself, he imagined data entry to be an awful lot like Jesus' carpentry trade). He'd overheard enough conversations to know his coworkers thought it absurd he consulted the Lord whenever he found a numerical inconsistency he couldn't solve on his own. But the Bible commanded the church to rely on God's wisdom rather than the wisdom of men, and so far, in Alan's experience, the Lord's wisdom had never failed. Still, he wasn't popular at work; his boss had even requested he take down the scriptures he'd tacked to the walls of his cubby, stupidly alleging they violated the other workers' First Amendment rights. "Your request violates *my* First Amendment rights," Alan had answered. But this was how it was forecast to be in the last days. And with the Lord's arrival imminent, he needed to bear witness. So he didn't take the scriptures down. Instead, he hung a new one from the fifth chapter of Matthew:

> *Blessed are they which are persecuted for righteousness sake, for theirs is the kingdom of heaven. Blessed are ye when men shall revile you and persecute you and say all manner of evil against you falsely for My sake. Rejoice and be exceedingly glad: for great is your reward in heaven: for so persecuted they the prophets which were before you.*

Alan ran a soapy sponge over each car. He'd taken today and tomorrow off to pray over Rachel's early return and to help the pastor devise a new plan. The largest portion of his desire for Rachel's repentance concerned leaving his miserable day job to propose becoming Pastor Lou's assistant pastor at church. He'd planned to do this for years, before Rachel's recent announcement. The pastorship would pay poorly but would offer the non-material riches of working for the Lord, the church, and Pastor Lou. But having a faithful, involved wife would be an implicit job requirement. A pastor's wife had to be available in a multitude of ways. And Rachel, as she was, did not seem fit. If she were fully repentant, perhaps the church would accept her. Even Pastor Lou said Rachel may not be fully accountable for the abortion, as she was still a child when it happened. Still, Alan knew she had been old enough to know better, and her lack of repentance, he was sure, had prevented her from conceiving in their three years of marriage, though she and Alan had been trying.

He hosed down each car and began on the wax. He lamented the task was almost finished and he'd soon have to return to the house where Rachel's presence made the very air feel heavy and grim. He imagined their lives stretching forward year after year in this manner. Something had to change, he prayed. In answer, Alan saw the face of Jesus Christ in his car's driver side mirror. *Trust in Me*, the vision of Jesus said.

Immediately, Alan knelt on the driveway, his knees in a runoff of soapy water, his forehead on the wet asphalt. When his visions crossed the chasm between the spiritual and material worlds, he understood best what King David wrote in the book of Psalms: "Let all the earth fear the Lord: let all the inhabitants of the world stand in awe of Him." You think your life is made of mundane and unfrightening things, like cars and houses and day jobs at computers until God's *true* world perforates the realm of daily life, disrupting and minimizing everything you thought was real. How awe-inspiring it must have been when the Lord made Himself known in the time of David, or even in Jesus' time when, according to Pastor Lou, people believed the earth to be a flat thing afloat in a vast body of water. Even prophets must have feared God's glory would destroy the earth. When the heavens opened and God's holy light shone down on Saul, for example, as he walked the road to Damascus, did he worry a vast sea would pour through the opening? Did he close his eyes in anticipation of another great flood? And when he opened his eyes and found himself blind, did he think the communion between the two worlds had lit and then extinguished the whole earth?

On the driveway, his clothes and hands and face wet, Alan meditated on that verse from Psalms.

"Lord," he prayed, "I give You my awe." He looked at the mirror again, but the Lord's face had gone. Instead, he heard the Lord's quiet voice in his ear. *Trust in Me,* it said again. *Fast and pray.* And Alan rejoiced.

He would not tell anyone except the pastor that the Lord had appeared to him again, this time in the car mirror. Once, at work, he had seen the Lord's face in his computer screen. When he'd called a coworker, the face disappeared, perhaps leaving Alan looking delusional. *Do not tempt the Lord your God,* the Lord's voice had reminded him as his coworker stood smirking.

Alan was only seven years old the first the Lord blessed him with a vision. He still remembered the long-sleeved brown shirt he wore, the one with the stripes. His mother had bought it for him and he'd liked its soft fabric. One evening after dinner, his father had banished him to his bedroom for some infraction he no longer considered important enough to remember. He'd sat on his bed in that soft, striped shirt and had looked at the clock to see how much time had passed. The face of Jesus stared back from the clock's face. It wasn't the face he'd seen sculpted in plaster and mounted on the crucifix that hung at the front of his parents' church. His father looked a bit like that version of Jesus, with red-brown hair, pale skin, and a scraggly beard. This face was darker, the hair and beard were black and curly, the eyes dark brown but bright with love. Although unlike any rendering of Jesus he had ever seen, Alan recognized Him instantly. He called for his mother, wanting for her to see Jesus, too, but when she arrived, His face had gone. "It was just a daydream," his mother said, at which Alan began to cry. Misunderstanding, his mother promised, "I'll take the clock down, Sweetie. No one's there. You don't have to be afraid." She carried it from Alan's room. Afterward, Alan made a paper sign that read "Thank You, Jesus" to hang in the clock's vacated place.

He still had that paper sign—laminated now—hanging in the bedroom where Rachel, presently, had barricaded herself. He liked to look at the inept, childish penmanship and bright crayon colors that mirrored the love, joy, and clean, new salvation he felt that day.

After the Lord's face appeared to him in the clock, Alan began to see it other places: in traffic lights, puddles, or even cooking pots. Now, he thought these sightings seemed comical when compared to the burning bushes and blinding lights of the Bible; prophecy in modern times seemed to take more quotidian forms. But before Eve was beguiled by the serpent and persuaded Adam to sin, Adam also saw God in quotidian ways. In the evenings, God and Adam would walk together in the garden; if Adam had possessed cars and clocks, Alan thought, he doubtless would have seen God reflected there. And seeing Jesus in the car mirror was not unlike experiences of some of the minor Biblical figures, like Balaam, to whom the Lord spoke via the mouth of a donkey.

The house was dark in comparison to the bright outdoor light; Rachel was still holed up in the bedroom, her absence much more noticeable than when she'd been gone altogether. He would make dinner for her, Alan decided. He was fasting, but she would need to eat. He had planned to maintain the house while Rachel was gone, to cook and to clean and to do the shopping; those domestic duties, he thought, would feel like bright spots in his days. He often helped with the chores and cooking anyway, not wanting to be a man like his father who expectantly cried out, "Iron me a shirt" whenever he needed one and who didn't even know how to make toast.

They still had chicken breasts and vegetables that Rachel had bought at the grocery store last week. He cooked for her, hoping she would smell the chicken baking and come out, sparing him the awkward humiliation of knocking on his own bedroom door.

She could eat her meal and they would pray. But she didn't come out, so he prepared a plate for her and carried it down the hall.

"We need to pray," he said though the door. "I've got dinner."

He heard a loud sigh, the rustle of bedclothes, and heavy footsteps toward the door. Rachel looked so angry when the door opened. "I said I wasn't hungry."

Alan handed the plate to her anyway, relieved that she reached for it.

"I won't eat it," she said.

"That's all right," Alan answered. "You can just keep it next to you when we pray. You might want it after."

She placed it on the bedside table. "I won't want it," she said.

"We need to pray, Rachel."

"Not now," she repeated. "Please."

"Why are you angry?"

"Why?" She shook her head as though in disbelief. "I want to make a phone call," she said. "Please."

She closed the bedroom door again. He heard the tones of push buttons and Rachel's voice, but her words were too quiet to decipher. Perhaps she'd called the pastor, he thought, or the pastor's wife, but soon he Amy's name. He didn't understand. He wanted to break down the door and demand to know to whom she was speaking. But he knew he needed to stay calm. Jesus overturned the merchant tables in the temple out of righteous anger because people were defiling a sacred place. His anger, he knew, was simply a reaction to feeling left out.

He would go for a walk around the neighborhood. He would pray.

Outside in the dinnertime quiet, kids' bicycles stood in driveways, not yet put away for the night, positioned as though their riders had quickly dismounted when called in to eat. Automatic sprinklers watered some of his neighbors' lawns and everything smelled scrubbed. Soon the children would come back out to play games with code words and flashlights until their mothers called their names. In a week or so, they'd all go back to school. After dinner, they'd probably be settling down to their homework.

He was blessed, inordinately blessed, to live here in Riverview. As a child, he'd lived in Northern New Jersey with his parents. His father worked at the Pepsi plant, and his mother stayed home with him. But they'd moved to Riverview, where the real estate was cheap, when Alan was nine or ten. His father had called it "a ridiculous, one-horse piney town"—a true enough assessment but not the whole truth. Yes, Riverview had once been populated with chicken farms and pine trees, but by the time Alan's family arrived, low-cost houses and a few department stores had replaced the coops and trees and farms. His parents bought a four-bedroom ranch for forty-five thousand dollars. They'd sold it for nearly five times that amount years before, taking the profit and moving to Florida, far enough away from New Jersey that Alan was spared the obligation of all but occasional visits. Alan's house was smaller than his parents' had been. It was a manufactured home in one of Riverview's most affordable developments these days, and it stood on a tiny plot of land that had once been a swamp. All along the street stood other manufactured homes. The house sometimes seemed to disappoint Rachel, but Alan didn't mind. The Word said to owe no man anything, and the house was completely paid for. He didn't need anything fancier. A mansion awaited him in Heaven.

Alan often marveled that, just as the Lord had engineered Jesus' birth in a stable in Bethlehem, He had installed Pastor Lou and his living, powerful church here in the humble remnants of Piney country, rather than in New York or Philadelphia, which stood less than an hour-and-a-half away in either direction. When he and his parents had first moved here, Alan had accompanied them to their small Episcopal church every Sunday morning. Even today, his parents remained practicing Episcopalians ("the frozen chosen," Pastor Lou called them) and professed to be unable to understand why Alan had joined a church that held five-hour services and only offered Holy Communion once a month.

But his parents had never understood the special friendship Alan had enjoyed with the Lord ever since the Lord first appeared to him, nor that this friendship, during Alan's childhood, felt strongest when he was alone, praying and reading the Bible, not during the dull rituals happening in his parents' church. Pastor Lou, later, drew Alan's attention to Jesus' words in the Gospel of Mark. Jesus had explained that religious traditions "nullified the Word of God," and that many who considered themselves religious "reject the Commandments of God so as to hold the traditions of men." So it was, Alan thought, with his parents.

Pastor Lou's church was different. He'd met the pastor at the Boardwalk when he was sixteen years old. There was no river in Riverview, but the Atlantic Ocean was merely one town east, a fifteen minute drive across the bridge at the end of the highway. The Boardwalk adjacent to the beach comprised a couple of miles of wooden planks held together with bolts and tar and populated with games of chance and carnival rides. Every Memorial Day through Labor Day during high school, Alan worked there as children's ride operator.

Even those years ago, the Boardwalk attracted a dubious crowd. Teenagers came to walk the strip in search of liquor and easy sex. Some adults came looking to buy or sell drugs. Meanwhile, families who couldn't afford trips to Disney World or even to Atlantic City tried in vain to have a wholesome time among the unfriendly, misbehaved locals. (The Boardwalk had grown worse recently. Alan heard there was a stand near the kiddie rides at which teenagers could get their privates pierced.) When he first saw the pastor, Alan had been standing at his ride ("The Bug Buggy"—a chain of twelve, slow moving little bug-shaped cars, each fitted with a seat, seatbelt, and ineffectual steering wheel in the middle of which, unfortunately, sat a button for the young passenger to press to create a loud, mosquito-like buzzing noise. Each car's button created a buzz of a slightly different pitch. Sometimes, Alan would hear their echoes for hours after work). He was collecting tickets, checking kids' seatbelts, and smelling the Boardwalk air, a mixture of early summer, tar, and pizza sold by the slice at Lucky Leo's Arcade.

Pastor Lou and some of the other church members

wore white t-shirts emblazoned with the message "Jesus Lives." Even at a distance, Alan could see the pastor's vibrant, earnest face and yearned to join him. He remembered that, in the Gospels, Jesus approached James and John while they fished and promised to make them "fishers of men." They abandoned their nets and became Jesus' disciples. On his break, Alan patrolled the Boardwalk, looking for that group in white t-shirts. He found them standing alongside a fence that separated the Boardwalk from the beach. Pastor Lou preached into a megaphone, his voice overpowering the rock music coming from a bar on the pier and the screams issuing from roller-coaster riders. Alan listened to the pastor's words, and even though he'd never seen anyone do it, closed his eyes, lifted his arms in the air, and began to praise the Lord aloud. Today, this action was so ordinary that he sometimes took it for granted. But that night, his arms felt as though they were a funnel through which the Lord's spirit could be poured directly from Heaven into his body.

While he stood praising the Lord, a teenage couple approached the group. They had their hips pressed together and their hands in one another's back pockets. Even now, many years later, Alan remembered the black t-shirts they wore and the boy's grin when he raised his pinky and forefinger. Alan could feel the Devil working behind the boy's eyes and hollered, "Satan, I cast you out in the precious name of Jesus," and the boy had started weeping, right there on the Boardwalk.

Pastor Lou had come over then, laying hands on the boy and on Alan. The boy got saved and the pastor told Alan, "You have a tremendous calling on your life." And Alan knew it was real. That Sunday, Alan attended Pastor Lou's church for the first time. It was a smaller congregation then, tucked away in an old farmhouse, but the Lord's presence was alive and enormous, and Alan never looked back.

For hours, Alan walked, praising the Lord. The evening grew steadily darker, the crickets and locusts made their voices heard, and the windows of the neighborhood houses glowed yellow with light. Here and there, American flags hung on porches, leftovers from the Gulf War, four years ago. The Word had prophesied "wars and rumors of wars" in the Last Days, and Alan was sure the Rapture would come within his lifetime. If Rachel would repent, he could be made assistant pastor. If she would repent, he could prepare the way for the Lord full time, just as John the Baptist once did.

When he got home, they would pray together.

But his house was dark by the time he finally returned. He tapped on the bedroom door.

"Are you ready to pray, Rachel?" he called quietly.

The door opened. She was dressed for bed. "Let's pray in the morning," she said. "Please."

"Pastor Lou told me that we need to spend the night in prayer," Alan explained. "If you're going to be here, we need to pray now."

"No," she answered. "What we need, honestly Alan, is to be quiet together. We need to be able to hold each other without asking God or… or the pastor for permission first."

He stared at her. "Then tomorrow morning, at 8:00, we have a meeting with Pastor Lou," he finished.

"If you love me," she continued, "you'll listen to me. I don't need to pray and I don't need the pastor. I need you to act like you love me."

"Come on," he said. "That's the flesh talking."

"The flesh?" she repeated. "It's *me* talking. Me. Not the flesh. Please, Alan, can't we just use our own words? Real words for awhile?"

"Pastor Lou wants us to pray," he said again. "Then in the morning, he'll help us figure out someplace else where you can go, a different ministry."

"A different *ministry*? For what? Some fetus that never existed?" She shook her head. "All I did was tell a lie. That's all I did. And you want me to go to some other Jesus Jail? You think God lives in these places? He wouldn't set one foot in them."

He didn't know what to believe. Was this one of the new, intractable demons? He'd never known Rachel to lie. "Rachel," he said. "I have to obey the pastor. I have to obey God."

"You think this is God?" she asked. "Sending me away like some teenager? Like the Rotolos sent Amy away? You really think this is God?"

"Yes," Alan answered.

"Not my God," she said.

The world's standards of right and wrong were so different from God's, Alan thought. The world might say he had been wrong to send Rachel away, just as it might say the Rotolos were wrong to reject Amy. But to obey God, to do what was right in His eyes, he'd simply had no other choice. And it wasn't as though he'd stopped thinking about Rachel. For three solid days, he had prayed for her without ceasing. Pastor Lou had told him, "Stand in the gap for her," and he had; he had stood in faith for her repentance. He would do it again. He was doing it now. "I'm standing in the gap for you, Rachel," he said. "I really am."

"What gap?" she replied. "There's no gap." And she slammed the bedroom door.

***

Not knowing what else to do, Alan settled down to sleep in the guestroom. The sheets on the bed felt stiff, as though they'd just been removed from their packages. No one had ever slept in this bed. Years of marriage and they'd never had an overnight guest. The mattress crinkled beneath Alan's weight. He shifted, trying to get comfortable.

She'd wanted him to *hold* her? Without praying first? To hold her body close to his without first discerning and casting out the spirits she'd brought home with her? Even when the situation was less dangerous, her body's expressions of affection seemed false and crude compared to the pure spiritual communion Alan enjoyed with the Lord. One night, early in their marriage, Rachel had looked at him quizzically, as if she'd never seen him before, and had asked, "Do you love me?"

"Of course," Alan had answered.

"But do you *love* me?" she'd repeated.

"Of course," he'd said again. But he knew why she'd asked twice. Jesus had once asked Simon Peter, "Do you love Me?" with "love" as *agape* in the Greek translation, meaning, do you love Me beyond the level of feelings. Do you love Me with your spirit? But, in the Greek translation, Peter had answered, "You know

I *phileo* You" which meant that he loved Jesus like a brother. So Jesus repeated the question. He wanted to make it clear that brotherly love was not enough. He demanded the kind of love that God demanded. He demanded it from His disciples and He demanded His disciples offer it to one another.

With Rachel, the conversation seemed to work in reverse. She was asking for Alan to love her with his feelings, and even worse, with his body, as though loving her with his spirit, on the level of the spirit, was less beautiful instead of more. Alan had felt betrayed when Rachel asked him to choose the flesh's version of love over the spirit's. "Of course," he had answered, hoping that one day, he and Rachel would transcend into the pure, deep compassion and fellowship of *agape* love. At the time, he thought the love they shared for Christ would help them get there. But it seemed they had not gotten there, and he worried that no feelings at all could remain between them.

He lay in the guestroom bed, unsure what to pray. Should he pray for Rachel's repentance? Should he pray for her *agape* love? Should he pray for the release of her demons? He closed his eyes and heard the Lord's distinct, quiet voice. Again, it said, *Trust in Me.*

Alan thought again of the crayon sign he'd made as a child when the Lord first appeared to him. At the Lord's gentle urging, he unearthed some paper and crayons from the kitchen junk drawer and wrote, "Jesus Loves You" over and over again in multiple colors. He hung the signs in every room and hid them in the house's most traveled spots: the refrigerator, the linen closet, the drawer where they kept their keys, and atop the butter dish. Finally, he went back to the guestroom and fell gratefully asleep.

When he woke early the next morning, Alan immediately noticed his hunger. It occurred to him that the Lord had never before asked him to fast, and that this new sacrifice was more uncomfortable than he would have expected. He felt light-headed when he stood, and the floor seemed to shift beneath his feet. The door to the master bedroom stood open.

"Rachel?" he called. "We have to be at church in an hour."

She didn't answer.

"Rachel?" The drawers on her side of the dresser were only partly closed; many clothes, Alan could tell, had been removed, and those that remained looked as though a burglar had rifled through them. Only a few of Rachel's old shirts hung in the closet and great patches of dust on the night tables marked the places where framed, individual photos of her mother and father had once stood. Apparently, Rachel had ransacked the entire room for every scrap of herself. He didn't need to look outside to know her car would be gone. He made his way into the kitchen. She had obviously discovered the notes Alan had left. They were piled on the table; a rock weighted them down.

How could he have slept while, overnight, she packed her things and drove away? He had done everything the Lord had told him to. How could this be the outcome? He removed the rock from the table and, without expecting to, threw it at the kitchen window.

***

Even on weekday mornings, Pastor Lou's church bustled. The building overlooked the highway, its exterior walls painted to proclaim, "He is Risen!" in large, bold letters. Though his hands had been shaking on the steering wheel, Alan felt calmer when he read that message. How beautiful to be redeemed by Jesus' blood. Alan thought of Pastor Lou's fervent occasional declaration from the pulpit, "The world thinks we're crazy." It occurred to Alan that "the world" might very well include Rachel. "Not my God," she had said. Well, who *is* your god, then?

He pushed open the sanctuary's whispering front

doors. In his hunger and despair, he noticed the peaceful beauty of the church anew. He'd never felt at home in any other building. In this church, the walls felt permeable as skin, membranes that let in the Lord but kept out the Devil. Here, the humiliations looming so large behind other walls—humiliations of sex and marriage and the world's definitions of right and wrong—seemed to dissipate. The largest problems of Alan's life diminished instantly and rose, as specks of dust, away from him to the church's vaulted ceiling. Here, life's only meaningful details pertained to sin and the absence of sin, because in the absence of sin, he could feel the love of the father and His son, Jesus Christ, Alan's Lord and savior.

The pastor's office door was closed. Even though he was early for their meeting, Alan knocked and waited. When he opened the door, Pastor Lou smiled.

"Praise the Lord," the pastor said, extending his arms in welcome.

"Praise the Lord," Alan answered.

The pastor grinned at Alan. Then, soberly, he asked, "Where's Rachel?"

"She's gone," Alan replied. "She left in the middle of the night."

"Come in."

Shaken and hungry though he was, Alan couldn't

help admiring the little office. Concordances, Bibles, Greek and Hebrew translation dictionaries, and even a copy of the latest Christian paperback thriller *The Apocalypse Fighters* lay on the desk alongside scraps of paper bearing the pastor's crimped handwriting.

"Did you pray with her?"

Alan shook his head.

The pastor looked surprised. "We talked about that," he said.

"I wanted to pray with her." Alan defended himself. "I told her we needed to. She wouldn't pray. I slept in the guestroom. I didn't hear her go."

"She'll come back, Alan. She won't be gone long."

"She took all her things."

"She'll come back," he repeated.

"She says it didn't happen, you know."

"Yes, I've heard that's the line she's taking. Did you check it against your spirit?"

"Did you?"

"Of course. And I think you should too. The Devil is doing a job on her."

"She says I don't love her because I sent her away."

Pastor Lou laid a hand on his shoulder. "If we didn't love her, it wouldn't matter to us if she got right with God. You have to trust Him."

Alan nodded. "That's what He keeps telling me. I saw Him in the car mirror yesterday."

"Hallelujah," Pastor Lou said. "Let me show you something." In the corner of the room, the screensaver on the computer scrolled the text: "This is the day that the Lord has made. I will rejoice and be glad in it." The pastor had purchased this oversized trainwreck of a machine just months ago, after Alan had been the first person to ever tell him about the internet. If Alan were assistant pastor, he'd be sure to help Pastor Lou choose better equipment and to learn this new technology that the apostasy would surely use one day soon. The pastor jiggled the mouse and a webpage slowly brightened the screen. The page showed a photograph of an armored tank. Alan stared at it, unsure.

"Tank of the Israeli Army," the pastor said. "Do you know what they call it? The Merkava."

"Ezekiel's Chariot," Alan said. He could almost hear John the Baptist explaining the merkava to Jesus and wished he too were beside the Jordan River, thinking of the chariot and preparing to be purified by John.

"Set your affection on things above today, Alan," the pastor said. "And trust Him. I'll make some calls. He's a merciful God. She'll have another chance."

***

He considered going home; perhaps Rachel had already come back and needed him. But he dreaded the confrontation that would follow. He would set his affection on things above instead. He thought of the merkava. Seated in the sanctuary, Bible in hand, he read and reread the tenth chapter of Ezekiel, then closed his eyes, meditating on the four faces and four wings of the four cherubim at the chariot's four wheels. He wanted to see the chariot descend there, right there, in the middle of the sanctuary. He wanted to see the angels' human-looking hands beckoning him from under their wings. How blissful to board that chariot and to have it bear him to Heaven.

Get baptized again, Alan heard the Lord say. The church had a baptismal for use when the weather was cold, but John used "living waters," not oversized bathtubs. His disciples sat on the river banks, listening to John's teachings, eating locusts and wild honey. He would get baptized in living waters, too, he decided. He would drive to the ocean.

Outside, the day was cool, and the winds promised autumn. He parked next to the pier and walked along the Boardwalk awhile; he passed the stands, his old workplace—that ride had been replaced by an even noisier one—and the first place he'd ever seen the pastor. The salty, fishy, moist air clung to his face. A trace of gentle, piping carousel music made itself heard amid the racket of the ocean's crashing waves. To his west, the tourist neighborhood had an exhausted, end-of-season look. To his east, only a few people walked in the wind on the beach. He jumped from the Boardwalk onto the cool sand.

He was hungry.

Sing to Me, Alan heard the quiet voice of the Lord command and Alan lifted his voice in song. He sang in Tongues first, his voice dissipating quickly into the rough ocean breeze; then a new song began. It was "Jesus Loves Me," which he hadn't sung since he was a child. He walked across the beach and kept singing.

"Jesus loves me; this I know, for the Bible tells me so. Little ones to Him belong. They are weak, but He is strong."

He reached the ocean, spotted a few intrepid swimmers in the distance, and waded forward into the cold, cold waves. The seaweed clung to his ankles, and he struggled forward, the water heavy against his legs and filling his shoes, the ocean floor gripping his feet, the undertow tugging him sideways.

"Yes, Jesus loves me. Yes, Jesus loves me."

When John first baptized Jesus, the heavens opened and the voice of God called down, "This is My beloved son in whom I am well pleased." Alan pushed farther until the water reached his waist. He'd cut his ankles on shells and debris, and the salt stung these new scratches as he stood and shivered, looking out into the farthest reaches of the brown-green Atlantic, then at the sky. He saw no clouds. He would be warmer, he thought, once he wet his head. "Baptize me, Father God," he prayed before ducking into the murk. When he ran out of breath, he lifted his head, salt on his lips, grit and sand up his nose and in his hair. The residual water on his eyelashes served as a kind of prism, and, in the sky, Alan saw the outlines of four wheels and, attached to each wheel, cherubim with four faces and four wings. He raised his voice in song.

"Yes, Jesus loves me. The Bible tells me so."

Eyes on the merkava, Alan found it easier to walk into deeper water, the waves washing over his head, the Lord's strength in his legs, the Lord's voice merging with his own as he sang and sang, stopping only when he needed to expel the pungent, fishy ocean water from his mouth.

You are the bride of Christ, he heard the Lord tell him again and again. *Fast and pray but don't despair your worldly marriage. Set your affection on things above, not on things of this earth. For soon, you will join Me at the feast I've made for you, a true wedding feast.*

Alan could not guess how much time he spent in the Atlantic, praising God, watching the chariot above him radiate its awesome power. Finally, the sky grew grayer and the chariot disappeared. He walked heavily back toward the beach, trying to reorient himself. The undertow had carried him far from where he'd started. By the time he returned to the car, his clothes and hair were stiff with salt water and seaweed and sand, and he couldn't stop shivering with cold and hunger and joy. Rachel would be home by now. By now, she would have talked to Pastor Lou. By now, she would have agreed to pursue a second chance. And before she could leave for the new ministry Pastor Lou would have found, Alan would tell her about the merkava, the wedding feast, and the love of Christ. He would remind her where to set her affection.

But as he drove across the bridge spanning the bay that separated Riverview from the ocean-side towns, as he watched the streetlights respond to the encroaching dusk, Alan's prophetic sense prickled with dread and foreboding.

Colder and hungrier and more nervous than he could ever remember being, Alan prayed for strength and calm. He drove through his housing development, past houses lit and closed for the night. A car that wasn't Rachel's waited in the driveway outside his dark house, and leaning against the car stood the shadowy outlines of a woman and a child.

He parked at the curb and approached the figures,

his wet shoes noisy.

"You're soaked!" the woman said. It was Lee.

"I was baptized," Alan told her. "I saw the merkava."

"They're both gone," Lee answered. "I think they're together. I don't know where."

"I know," said Alan because he was not the least surprised. "Come inside," he said.

Lee shook her head. "Do you have any idea where they'd go?"

"No." His cold fingers struggled with his key ring, trying to isolate the house key.

"I told him to take Rachel and go," Lee said. "We were fighting so much. But I didn't mean for him to do it. He left in the middle of the night. I really didn't mean for him to do it if he didn't want to."

"Let me get in some dry clothes," he said. "I'll make us some tea and we'll pray."

Again, Lee shook her head. "There's nothing to pray for," she said. "He wanted to go. I guess they both wanted to."

"Set your affection on things above," Alan said. He felt as though ice filled his whole body.

"I didn't mean for it to happen," Lee said again.

"Come inside, Lee. Let's give it to God."

"I need to get back home."

"Listen," Alan began, but he didn't know what to

say next. It seemed important to tell her something, to make her understand. "We're the bride of Christ," he said. "We'll be present at the wedding feast. Set your affection on things above."

"Oh, Alan." She lifted Justine, kissed the top of the child's head, and situated her into one of those hopelessly complicated safety seats.

"It's Colossians 3:2," Alan added.

"Yes." Lee looked at him. "I grew up in Christian foster homes, you know. Sometimes we had to recite scriptures in order to earn our dinner. That one's a favorite. But what about verse 19?"

"19?"

"Look it up," Lee said. "And go get warm. You're going to get sick."

Shivering, Alan watched her drive away.

Inside, he turned on the heat for the first time in months; the forced air smelled dusty and close. A cold draft took advantage of the hole he'd made in the kitchen window. He sat on the kitchen floor in his wet clothes, sand falling from his pants and skin, and pressed his body against the heating vent. How often he had done this as a child when his father or mother had left the house, propelled by a seemingly endless rage. How often he had curled against a heating vent, praying.

He opened his Bible to Colossians 3:19. It read, "Husbands love your wives, and be not bitter against them."

The words swam. No. He would set his affection on things above. "What do I do, Lord?" he asked.

Trust in Me, the Lord reminded him.

"I'm weeping with rejoicing, Lord," Alan prayed aloud.

PITCH

Lee dipped a cleaning rag into a bucket of warm water, the soap oily against her skin, and washed one of the store's baby grand pianos, a highly polished cherry-wood; the golden letters embossed above the keyboard announced the brand name Young Chang. She remembered, as though from another life, how happy Paul's father had been when he'd landed the Young Chang line for the franchise of stores he owned. Piano brands, apparently, had territories, much in the way of drug dealers. The musical instrument superstore on the highway had already claimed Yamaha's local turf, and Paul's father had needed a comparable product to stay competitive. Lee finished washing the cherry-wood piano and moved on to another, a glossy black upright Wurlitzer from the store's economy line. Pastor Bianchi's wife was right; it helped to have a task.

Once she finished the pianos, she'd dust the grandfather clocks and ostentatious figurines. Paul had only recently begun selling Italian collectibles in the store he managed for his father: gaudy ceramic statuettes and fiberglass flowers. "What are these doing here?" Paul's father had ostensibly asked upon initially eyeing a shelf full of tall, nostalgic hand-painted clowns. "You don't want this to turn into a junk shop." But Paul's store was situated in the mall of one of those retirement villages that seemed to be cropping up all over Riverview, and the figurines, Paul said, enchanted many of the old lady shoppers so much that they stopped in several times a week to inquire about new merchandise.

Today, when the store opened, Lee would have to hope for customers and to try to make a sale. Paul's father would come to teach her how. She'd do this every weekday until Paul came back—*if* he came back—from wherever he and Rachel had gone. "I'm sorry, Paul," she said aloud. His face made itself present in her imagination. It was kissing Rachel's face. Yes, it seemed probable he would never return.

The gate to the store's front entrance was still closed, but Lee could see through its metal chinks. Across the wide courtyard shone a bakery's pink neon sign. Next to the bakery stood a store called Comfy Duds. The local group of mall-walkers—seniors from the residential village who got daily morning exercise by walking the mall's corridors—had already passed the store twice. The pastor and his wife had joined them today even though they didn't live here and looked more spry than those who did. They were walking hand-in-hand with Lee's daughter. Watching them, Lee could almost feel the spongy thickness of Justine's hand and resented that the Bianchis had the right to touch her. Would Paul and Rachel wind up with Justine? She pictured members of the church smiling at redressed wrongs. Paul's parents, the pastor and his wife, and even Alan would probably agree that Paul and Rachel needed to become a family with a child. And here was Justine, helplessly available for the taking.

Lee carried the cleaning bucket into the dingy bathroom at the back of the store. Blue-black stains marked the toilet and sink.

In the mall, old-fashioned calliope music piped through hidden speakers. Lee remembered that Paul's father had instructed her to overpower the mall's music with the store's own. In the very front of the store stood an organ that could be programmed to play autonomously. She hit the button marked "demo." Without inflection, the organ blared a synthesized version of "La Bamba." Lee sat heavily on the organ bench.

Three days since Paul left and this was where Lee found herself. Could it be real? Yes, there were the mall-walkers shuffling past in their old people shoes, and there was Justine, one hand wrapped around the pastor's thumb, the other waving. "Hi, Mommy."

"We go around one more time," Mrs. Bianchi shouted.

Lee nodded. "Have fun."

At 10:00, immediately after Lee had raised the gate, an old woman pushing a little cart stepped over the store's threshold. Lee glanced down and noticed an oxygen tank. She felt her lungs constrict, as if in anticipation of her own infirm years. "Are there any new dolls?" the woman asked in a whisper that sounded as though it required all her effort. She wore a pink sear-sucker suit and thick-soled white shoes. Oxygen tubes dangled from her nose, obscuring her mouth.

"Dolls?" Lee repeated. She didn't know how Paul had done it, how he'd managed, day after day, to look at faces overrun by medical tubing. She was not as generous or as good as Paul.

The woman pointed to a shelf of figurines. "It's Monday. Nothing new?"

"No." Lee shook her head. "Paul isn't here."

She lifted her chin to indicate she hadn't fully heard. "Paul's sick?" she asked.

Lee nodded because it was easiest, but an uninvited

image of Paul as an old, ailing man flashed across her imagination. She wouldn't know him then. He would be Rachel's.

"He's coming back?"

Lee blinked furiously. "I don't know," she said. Then, for no real reason, she added, "I'm his wife."

She sized Lee up with yellow eyes. "You should be taking care of him," she said, pointing a spotted finger. "You should be home with him."

"I'm taking care of the store," Lee answered.

"It's all right for some," the woman said.

What's all right? Lee wondered, but she only turned toward the shelf in an attempt to look too busy to talk. She dusted the figurines for several moments until she finally heard the old woman's cart wheels click loudly over the threshold again. The statues showcased a melancholy Italian clown—the prototypical pagliaccio—in different poses of contemplation or entertaining. Lee dusted a clown who bowed low, offering a balloon to a little, black-haired girl whose hands were clasped coyly behind her back and whose eyes looked wise with adult sorrows. Lee stroked the girl's pouting, porcelain face. It looked like Rachel's.

"Good," Paul's father said, nodding at Lee as he came into the store through the back entrance. "Everything's clean. That's good."

"Good," Lee repeated. As always, Paul's father looked as though he'd just stepped off the set of an Italian movie. He wore tailored, linen slacks, a crisply pressed white shirt, a blue tie, and a tidy, off-white fedora. He took the hat off, rubbed a palm across his bald spot, and smiled. His smile looked so much like Paul's that Lee's hands momentarily shook. "The Bianchis and Justine are here," she said. "They're walking."

He looked at her as though trying to puzzle out what she'd meant, then nodded. "They have a car, you know."

"Yes," Lee answered.

"Come on," Paul's father said. "Let's get this done." He showed her where to find the receipts, the number to call to establish financing, and the credit card processor. "Let's see if you get any customers," he said, "and I'll talk you through a sale." He perched on a piano bench that faced the mall corridor and stared down at his hands. Lee sat beside him, ankles crossed, waiting. Apologies howled within her. A few ancient shoppers hobbled by slowly. The ones who stopped at the store inquired after the "dolls." No one seemed interested in buying instruments. She wished she had more pianos to clean.

"He should marry Rachel, don't you think?" she

asked without having meant to.

Paul's father still watched his fingernails; Lee noticed they were dented and ridged from years of having been bitten. He sighed.

"I wonder the pastor has got to," he said.

***

She'd met Rachel first, near the campus of Maranatha College, at the tea shop where Lee had begun working immediately after high school. Rachel, who attended the college, worked at the tea shop, too, and Lee, who was younger, who'd never been to college, who had no family, worshipped her instantly. Rachel told Lee about the poor kids from the city— "Fresh Air Fund kids"— who'd stay for weeks with families in her hometown every summer so they could swim and play outside. A couple of years later, when Rachel, about to graduate, told Lee her plan to return to Riverview, Lee, feeling rather like a Fresh Air Fund kid herself, begged to come.

Within a week, Lee found a job and a room to rent in Riverview, and until Rachel's mother died, followed Rachel everywhere. Half the town, it seemed, crowded into Rachel's childhood church after the Gulf War, as though to get in God's good books before more catastrophes could come, and Lee met everyone Rachel knew. Rachel had introduced Paul simply as "someone I went out with a long time ago" but, even then, Lee should have noticed the way Paul's eyes probably softened when he looked at Rachel. Then everything changed. Rachel's mother was dead; Rachel was dating Alan; and Paul, who often ate lunch at the Riverview café where Lee worked, had asked Lee whether she'd like to go out for dinner sometime. No one had ever invited her out for dinner before. There were boys in high school—some in the system, like her, and some not—who'd make out with her at parties or in the park, but no one took her anywhere. She knew, even then, that she wasn't the type of girl who deserved to be courted.

And Paul was so much more than she deserved: he asked her where she'd like to go and held doors for her when they got there. He sat beside her at church and handed her his Bible so she could find the passages they were asked to turn to during services. He introduced her to his parents and invited her to their house for Sunday dinners. So, at first, she didn't even think to complain when Paul spent their time together asking Lee what Rachel had said about him in the early days of her and Rachel's friendship, what she'd said about him after moving back to Riverview, and whether she thought Rachel was serious about Alan. Lee would spend hours listening to him, sympathizing with him, answering his questions as patiently as she could, and feeling fortunate to have his attention at all. And when he'd kiss her and say, "You're so sweet. You're such a good friend. I wish I could fall in love with you," she never considered walking away. Instead, she promised, "I'll earn your love," and hoped she'd one day be good enough to do so.

Sometimes, she even considered having sex with him. She'd managed to keep hold of her own virginity, despite considerable pressure from boys. It wasn't a choice based on her own faith; she'd never, after all, been able to fully believe in salvation or God or Jesus or the literalism of the Bible and had never even been able to support the ancillary doctrines of any church. To Lee, a fetus wasn't a human being, the earth wasn't six thousand years old, sex wasn't a sin, and people weren't sent to Hell because they believed in a god with a different name or set store by a different set of scriptures. But she was afraid, always, of losing what little she had, and every foster family and every foster family's church made their attitudes about pre-marital sex clear. Paul was the first person she'd dated after aging out of the system, and, for the first time, sex seemed a way to gain a family rather than a way to lose one. And she would have played that card, actually, if she'd known that he had once slept with Rachel. But, back then, even though she would have risked her own virginity in an attempt to win his love, she didn't feel entitled to ask Paul to waste his virginity on her.

So, instead, she compared herself to Rachel, part by part, trying to figure out what she could emulate. She knew she could never be loved, complete, and deserving like Rachel. Rachel, Paul often said, had been so romantic and mysterious that her very presence caused him to lose track of time. Lee knew she possessed no inner romance and was about as mysterious as a tomato. She could, however, work on her appearance. She'd never been beautiful, like Rachel, but she'd always been effortlessly, naturally cute; it was a liability, in fact, in foster care—making girls hate her and boys try to sneak into her room at night—but, compared to Rachel, she knew she looked rather plain. Rachel was a show pony—hair that she spent an hour curling each morning, more clothes than anyone needed, and so much mascara she always looked a bit as though she'd been shocked. Lee didn't know how to become that kind of girl, but she wanted to earn Paul's love, so she tried. She bought new clothes. She started wearing make-up. She learned to tweeze her eyebrows. And finally, a few days after Rachel and Alan announced their engagement, Paul looked at her and said, "You're very pretty, Lee. Do you know that?"

And sensing her opportunity at last, Lee said, "I don't think we should date anymore. I'll get married if you want to do that, but I don't think we should date."

"Let's get married, then," Paul said.

She expected marriage to make her feel more secure. She thought, once they were legally bound to one another, she wouldn't feel unhappy that Paul didn't love her. Sex, she thought, was the one thing she could give Paul that Rachel hadn't, and it would pass as love, wouldn't it? But the addictive newlywed sex she'd heard about—the very kind that had been promised as "worth waiting for" in abstinence sermons she'd heard at church when she was younger—never came. In bed, Paul seemed distant, uncertain, and disinvested. He didn't look at her. He didn't kiss her. Afterward, she'd roll onto her side, disconsolately lonely, thinking, "He doesn't want me." If she'd known, of course, that he'd already had sex with the woman he wanted, she might have gone mad with jealousy. And, in fact, she nearly had anyway. After the marriage, Rachel seemed to be an ever-present ghost, haunting Lee's thoughts and undermining her confidence. Instead of being Lee's friend, Rachel was the wife Paul should have had, the wife he'd truly wanted, the wife he'd have now if he weren't trapped in the marriage Lee had coerced him into.

Worse yet, once they were married, Lee could no longer keep quiet when Paul talked wistfully about Rachel. It was as though Lee had developed an allergy to even Rachel's name, and any mention of her old friend felt threatening to the fragile, taut security of her days. It got so bad that, once, when Justine was still an infant, Lee saw Rachel's car parked outside the Rotolos' house next door and became so convinced that Rachel had come to take Paul away that she had to hold the kitchen counter, to steady herself.

"She's married," Paul had told her that evening when they'd fought. "I wouldn't go."

And even though she hated herself for it, Lee had snapped, "You're married, too, Paul. Remember?"

***

The first twenty-four hours Paul was gone, Lee found that she couldn't hold on to the time that passed. Other people *did* something with their time, didn't they? But Lee had mostly sat on the couch, watching television. "Mommy's crying," Justine had said. "Mommy's crying." Her face was just like Paul's, Lee thought. It was as though her own genes had simply dissolved. Good, Lee thought. Better for everyone.

Paul had left in the middle of night. They'd been fighting; it had been her fault. But she'd expected him to come back. She'd sat on the couch for hours, waiting, the television on for noise. By the time Justine woke at dawn, Lee understood he was gone. She managed to leave the couch long enough to feed Justine and to bring a basket of stuffed puppies into the living room to keep her occupied. The daytime soap operas featured beautiful women, like Rachel, who cried over men, and the daytime talk shows featured ordinary-looking women, like Lee, who did the same thing. In the evening, Lee began to worry. What if Paul had been mugged? What if he'd been murdered? But when she called her mother-in-law, she learned that Rachel had disappeared overnight, too.

"We didn't want you to know," Paul's mother said. "The pastor didn't want me to tell you."

"Does Alan know?" Lee asked.

"He knows that Rachel's gone," Paul's mother said. "Don't tell him the other."

It wasn't fair, Lee thought. For years, she'd believed

that Paul and Rachel had never had sex. For years, Alan had probably thought the same thing. Why should she and Alan be protected from basic facts as though they were children? These were *their* marriages, not Paul's parents', not the pastor's. But when she finally drove to Alan's house, he quoted scriptures at her as though she hadn't told him anything at all. Rachel deserved someone better, Lee thought, driving home. Rachel deserved Paul. And she returned to the couch, Justine asleep on her lap. She stroked her daughter's hair and flipped through channels, stopping finally on an evangelist who preached about the Rapture.

It was a scary story, she thought. The first time she'd heard it, she was five or six years old and a foster mother had brought her to church for movie night. The film began by showing the main character, a woman who'd never gotten saved, waking up one morning to discover that her husband, a Born-again Christian, had been raptured. Tribulation began, she asked for salvation, went into hiding, and the end of the movie showed her, all in white, being led to a guillotine to be martyred with the other post-Rapture believers. Lee cried and cried. Then, just as the character reached the guillotine, just as the blade fell, she was suddenly at home again, in bed. Before Lee could relax, relieved the entire plot of the movie had been a dream, the camera revealed the husband's empty place. A song with the lyrics "would that we had all been ready" accompanied the end credits. Afterward, Lee practically ran to the altar for salvation, repeating the prayer she was told to repeat. All around her, people sobbed and shook and fainted and called out strange praises, but she just stood, head down, imagining herself in white robes, the blade quick and sharp against her neck.

"That was the most important opportunity of your lifetime," her foster mother told her afterward. "Make sure you make good on it."

"I will," Lee had promised, wanting to please. But soon she was passed to a new family and a new church. With each, she submitted to a new altar call and again asked for redemption. None of the families ever believed her when she told them she'd said the Sinner's Prayer before. But saying it, she knew, wasn't enough. The first half—the confession—was easy. She was told to "humble herself before God" and to confess her unworthy sinner's nature. She did it every time and believed every word she said. But the second half of the prayer—the request for and acceptance of salvation—stopped her. Salvation, literal or not, was not something she could ever deserve.

The television evangelist concluded his program

with a similar prayer, and Lee said the first half with him.

When late night commercials replaced programming, Lee half-heartedly thought of buying every product—the tooth whiteners and stomach slimmers and salad-makers and grills. Another kind of salvation, she thought; another way to try to become someone new. But she didn't deserve to be anyone new. Besides, she had no money. In the first year of her marriage, she'd waited tables, making sure to clock enough hours to bring home exactly as much money as Paul did, even during the pregnancy that happened so quickly after their wedding that everyone from church was probably counting the months on their calendars. When Justine was born, a month shy of her and Paul's first anniversary, Paul's parents insisted she stop working. It was scriptural, they argued. Paul didn't want her to—they needed her income—but his parents, as always, triumphed. And Paul's father, most clearly at Paul's mother's insistence, increased Paul's salary to, in Paul's words, "absorb the loss."

Lee understood herself to be the loss.

She watched commercials until the early morning news began and Justine awoke. Lee fed her daughter breakfast, took her to the bathroom—a tortuous one-hour process that involved much cajoling in the voices of stuffed dogs—and then, afterward, when it occurred to her she simply would not be able spend another hour that way today, found some leftover diapers and insisted Justine wear one. "Baby pants," Justine complained.

"When you can use the potty quickly like a big girl, you can go back to your big girl pants," Lee snapped. It was the cruelest thing she'd ever said to her daughter, and Justine cried in shock. Lee turned back to the television, eventually falling asleep. In her dreams, Rachel, taller and leaner than she really was, wore bright feathers braided into her long hair. Paul's mother applauded Rachel as she entered, and Lee's own mother, who'd been dead since Lee was four, stood, applauding too, beside Paul's. "I love her," Paul said to Lee, giving Rachel's arm a tender squeeze. "We all do." Lee woke at noon. Justine had obviously cried herself to sleep on the living room floor, a stuffed puppy beneath her cheek, bits of its toy fur stuck to the salty, smeared mess on her face. She had taken off the diaper. Restless, Lee paced the kitchen, filling the kettle, turning the burner on then off, looking aimlessly for something to eat, finding nothing, then returning to the couch.

During the second twenty-four hours, she managed somehow to make herself conscious of small events.

She found a can of Coke in the refrigerator, opened it, and after a sip, choked on its chalky sweetness. The can dropped from her hands and the Coke spilled, leaving an effervescent, brown, Alaska-shaped puddle on the kitchen floor. She swabbed the puddle with a paper towel but didn't wash the floor, and a sticky stain remained. The phone rang; she ran to it, breathlessly waiting to hear Paul's voice, but it was Mrs. Bianchi, offering a casserole and to take Justine for the afternoon or overnight. Lee watched Justine drape herself in some of Amy Rotolo's old baby blankets, which Mrs. Rotolo had given to Lee before Paul left. Justine wore the blankets as though they were gowns. Lee held Justine's warm hands. Waking up after a long nap, Lee found herself thinking, "There's no room, no room." Sweat soaked her shirt.

By the time she woke Sunday morning—yesterday—Paul had been gone for more than forty-eight hours. Sunlight streamed through the window, and the living room seemed strangely still and quiet. Sitting up, she noticed the overly warm indoor air stank of urine. Mrs. Bianchi stood beside the couch.

"You need to get up, Honey," she said. "Self-pity is a sin." Then she placed a bony, surprisingly gentle hand on Lee's forehead. "Your mother-in-law's depressed too, Honey," she said, "but she isn't lying around.

She's been at church. Interceding." Lee yielded to Mrs. Bianchi's authority and stood. The carpet bore urine stains, and Justine, whose shirt had not been changed and who had not been taken to the bathroom since Friday morning, sat in the corner, eyes closed, thumb in her mouth.

"Shower," Mrs. Bianchi said, handing Lee a great, mauve washcloth. "Then church."

Lee watched her own bare white feet carry her down the hallway and up the stairs, past more dried urine stains, and into the bathroom where the lavender ceramic tiles accosted her with their cheerful ignorance. In the shower, her feet looked rubbery and artificial at the ends of her legs. I have sexless feet, she told herself, sexless and ugly. What had Paul said about them? She couldn't remember. But once, she recalled, after he had asked her to rub *his* feet, he had instantly hollered, "Back off!" when she'd complied. That was long ago, when they'd first met, when simply looking at Paul made her feel as though her heart might pop with love.

Did she still love him?

The water beat horribly against her body, and she couldn't keep soap from getting in her eyes.

"I've got some clothes for you," Mrs. Bianchi said as she opened the bathroom door. "And I'm turning the fan on. It's steamy in here."

"Thank you." Lee washed her left forearm, rinsed it, and washed it again. It didn't make a difference, she told herself. Paul was the clean one. Well, Rachel and Paul. If Rachel and Paul lived here together, Lee told herself, this house would be clean and bright and happy, like those houses in television commercials. This was *already* Paul's house when Paul and Rachel were together, some malicious part of her brain agreed. Paul's parents had owned it all Paul's life, after all. When Paul and Lee got married, Mr. and Mrs. Esposito had sold it to Paul for almost nothing and had bought a bigger, nicer house around the block. Probably, Lee thought, this was the first place Paul and Rachel had ever made love. Probably, the house had felt much cleaner then.

Now, seemingly against her will, she considered whether Paul and Rachel had ever taken a shower together in this bathroom. As if in answer, their naked bodies seemed to stand with her, crowding her, stepping on her ugly, sexless feet so she couldn't walk away. They were teenagers, terrified, sneaking this shower while Paul's parents were out. Their ears attuned to any noise in the hallway, occasionally one or the other seemed to hear a mirage of Mrs. Esposito's voice and anxiously jutted a head into the cool bathroom air, listening. Then that same clean, youthful face reentered the shower's steamy world, and Paul and Rachel laughed, sharing relief and soapy kisses. Lee turned the water off. The phantoms lay on a towel spread across the bathroom floor. They've always been together, Lee told herself, walking around the clean, teenaged lovers. They always will be.

She took a breath and tried to force the past to fade. My bathroom, she said. My husband. My clothes. But none of these things, she knew, truly belonged to her. She regarded, for example, the outfit Mrs. Bianchi had hung on the towel rack. It was an outfit Paul's mother had given Lee last Christmas, and like most of Mrs. Esposito's presents to Lee, had more to do with Rachel's taste than Lee's. The blouse and skirt, made of stiff, robin's egg blue muslin, bore small decorative metal studs at the collar, cuffs, and hem. The blouse was to be worn tucked into the skirt, which was to be belted with a lace sash. "It was expensive," Mrs. Esposito had announced when Lee had opened the present. Paul and his father had cooed, "Isn't that beautiful?" and Mrs. Esposito, nodding vigorously, had added, "Lord and Taylor." She'd left the price tag on. The outfit had cost two hundred and twenty dollars. It was more than anyone should have spent on her, she knew, yet she also knew Paul's mother would have gladly spent double that on Rachel, and that Rachel would have deserved it much more.

Lee had admitted this, more or less, to Rachel. Rachel had arrived at the prayer meeting that started all this trouble just as Paul's mother had unearthed her newest insult—a Biblical coloring book about Jacob, who'd wanted to marry Laban's daughter, Rachel, but had been tricked into marrying Leah, Rachel's sister, instead. "It's just like you," Lee had told Paul. "Wanting Rachel but getting Lee."

"Don't start," Paul had answered. And it was such an unsatisfactory answer that, when Rachel arrived, Lee briefly remembered Rachel as her old friend and confidante and couldn't keep herself from showing her the coloring book, too. Just hours later, after Rachel had announced that she'd supposedly had an abortion, after Mrs. Esposito had hugged Lee the way Lee had always wished she would, after Paul had been scolded and shamed, and after Lee had finally learned the monstrous truth that Rachel and Paul had been lovers, not just childhood sweethearts, Rachel had looked at Lee and had asked, "Did that make it right?"

At home, afterward, she put Justine to bed, unusually declining Justine's nightly request that Lee narrate one of her stuffed dog's life stories, and then went into the room she shared with Paul. The house was dark except for the nightlight Justine claimed to need, which eked vague autumnal light into the hallway. Paul stood at the window, parted the heavy curtains, and looked into the night, seemingly toward the Rotolos' house next door. Lee didn't know whether to approach him. She didn't know whether she wanted to.

"I know why you didn't tell me," she said finally. Her voice sounded pinched and quiet. "You thought I'd have a jealous meltdown. And you were right."

"I didn't tell you because I didn't know," he answered.

"I mean about sleeping with her."

"It was such a long time ago."

Something ugly was building inside her, a closing, heavy darkness she used to feel, as a child, when she'd watch how her foster parents treated their biological children; those kids who, no matter how meager their skills, efforts, or accomplishments, would always be lauded by their parents for having great talents; those kids who, when no one else could hear, would threaten Lee with violence or mock her for anything they could think of, and yet who'd be exonerated by their parents if Lee dared to tell. "My daughter would never say that," the parents would claim, and Lee, chastised for lying when she hadn't lied, would feel herself losing ground. *My son. My daughter.* The words tortured her with the accuracy of their implications: She was nothing and deserved nothing, to be angry about it was shameful, and to ask for more, a crime. Still, she hoped.

She hoped even as she watched Paul's back, willing herself not to talk, not to start one of those fights that were beneath his dignity, and perhaps even her own. She hoped if she stayed quiet, he'd finally say the things she'd always needed to hear: that she belonged to him, that he loved her most of all, that he always would. "Please, God," she prayed silently. "I'll do anything. I'll give You anything."

But when Paul finally broke the silence, he only asked, "You don't think I'm a killer, do you?"

The closing darkness grew, rising into Lee's throat. "Over a fetus? Of course not. You know I don't feel that way about it." Then, as quietly as she could, she asked, "Do you think she was ever really pregnant?"

"No," Paul said. "I don't know."

She couldn't stop it. "That's worse then," she said. "If you'd told her to get rid of it, that you didn't want it, I'd be able to trust you again. But if you'd known, you would've married her, wouldn't you?"

"I don't know," Paul answered.

"And you would have been happy," Lee continued in that deadly quiet voice, hating this thing that overtook her, hating herself. "You were happier with her than you've ever been with me, weren't you?"

"Yes," he said.

"You loved her more."

"Yes," he said again.

"Then you are a killer."

"So are you," he replied.

***

Yesterday morning, in the outfit that ought to have been Rachel's, after brushing her teeth for the first time since Friday, Lee managed to work her way back down the hallway. Mrs. Bianchi, apparently, had cleaned. The hallway smelled of detergent, and parts of the carpet were stiff with drying suds. My house, Lee told herself, but another internal voice rose in contradiction. *Not yours*, it said. *Rachel's.* With every step, she felt as though phantoms of Rachel and Paul might rise through the carpet and tether her feet to the floor.

In the kitchen, she could hear the crunch of Justine's new, clean diaper as the child walked around. "You don't have to wear those baby pants," she told Justine.

"Yes I do," Justine answered.

"It seemed best," Mrs. Bianchi agreed. She handed

Lee a steaming cup. "It's coffee," she said. "I got it at the store on the way. I know Pastor says we shouldn't drink it, but I think it's OK today."

Lee sipped the coffee. It smelled of dead things. It wasn't Rachel's job to make things right, she told herself. Like Jacob, she'd simply claimed her birthright. Lee was the hairy, undeserving Esau. Lee, not Rachel, was the reason Paul went away.

Lee poured some cereal for Justine. Her eyes seemed foreign to Lee, slitted and wary. What was the point of having this child? What had she thought she'd accomplish? She loved the girl, but what did that matter? Once, long ago, when Paul had complained to her about his parents—their dominion over him, their ownership—she'd said, "At least they love you."

"You put too much emphasis on love," he told her. "You're too preoccupied with it. It doesn't guarantee anything." And she knew he was thinking of Rachel. But things had finally worked out for him, it seemed. He and Rachel would be together, and if they needed Justine, they would take her, too. No matter how much Lee loved her daughter, it guaranteed nothing.

"Eat your breakfast, Jussie," Lee said. She tried another sip of coffee.

"I have to go help Pastor get ready for service," Mrs. Bianchi said. "Your in-laws will come get you in their car."

"Car?"

"Church," Mrs. Bianchi reminded her. "You haven't been out all weekend."

"Right," Lee said. She thought of facing Paul's parents. They'd always known that she was trying to live a life that ought to have been Rachel's. But they'd managed, a lot of the time, to convey this through unspoken hints and subtle insults, in deference, she supposed, to the pretense she and Paul had been living. In a way, she thought, Rachel was almost entirely incorrect when she'd said that she'd made it right. Now everyone would feel free to say outright that Lee had no place here whatsoever.

It would be awful to lose her house and unimaginable to lose her husband and daughter. But it would be sad to lose the church, too. She'd always been sad to lose churches, sometimes even more than she'd been sad to lose foster families or schools. Apart from its general doctrine, she believed in the specific goodness of the church. Because churches, in her times of greatest need, had given her food and shelter, had encouraged foster parents to take her in, and had even served as places to make friends. As much as church after church ought to have turned her away for her insufficient faith, no church ever had. And even though she knew she was unworthy of welcome, she allowed it to happen, again and again.

"Church," Mrs. Bianchi repeated. "Then tomorrow you'll start working in Paul's store. Your father-in-law agreed to train you. It'll help. Having a task always helps."

***

So here she was, getting trained. Or, more accurately, she was waiting for a customer to arrive so training could happen.

"Did you bring your Bible?" Paul's father asked Lee.

"What?"

"I usually bring my Bible," he said. "That way, I can read when it's slow."

"Oh," Lee said. "I'll bring mine tomorrow."

Rachel would have brought her Bible, Lee thought. Rachel believed in God and, more significantly, believed that God gave a damn about her, that He *should* give a damn. Rachel probably believed she was going to Heaven someday. She probably believed she deserved to go. Well, Lee thought, if anyone deserved Heaven, Rachel did. Rachel's mother had been so immensely loved by her friends from church that they had actually considered trying to pray her back to life after she died. If Rachel were to die, Paul would probably lead the prayer himself.

"There they are!" Paul's father said, his face practically aglow with relief. The Bianchis and Justine had come into the store. Justine held an overlarge cookie the Bianchis had evidently bought from the bakery. "Did you have a good walk?"

"You know, Eddie, this place really has potential to grow into a ministry," Mrs. Bianchi answered. "These people are starving for the Word."

"Did the pastor buy you a cookie?" Lee asked Justine.

Justine smiled.

"She earned it," Mrs. Bianchi answered, winking at Justine. "She memorized all the Beatitudes on our walk. Go ahead, Baby, tell your mommy. Blessed are..."

"The merciful!" Justine exclaimed.

Paul's father glanced at Justine. "I can't understand it," he told the pastor. "I can't understand a thing he's done."

"We're all interceding for you, Eddie," Pastor Bianchi answered.

Paul's father nodded. "For the daughter-in-law too," he said.

"For the healing of all your family," the pastor said.

Lee felt that terrible darkness rise inside her again. "I don't want healing," she heard herself say. She lifted Justine onto her lap and kissed the child's silky, thin hair. Justine needed a bath, Lee noted.

"Take Justine," the pastor said, indicating his wife.

Mrs. Bianchi held her arms out to Lee's daughter. Then she put a hand on Lee's arm. "We're having a prayer meeting at our house tonight," she said. "Your mother-in-law will be there. You should come. It would be good for you."

"I don't want healing," Lee repeated. "I don't need it."

"The abortion probably did more harm to your marriage, in the spirit realm, than you can even imagine," Pastor Bianchi said.

You think the damage is in the spirit realm? Lee wanted to say. *You don't see the damage in this realm?* Instead she said, "The abortion probably didn't even happen. He loves her. I knew that and I married him anyway. I thought I could earn his love, but I couldn't because I wasn't enough. *That's* what did it."

"Of course it happened," Paul's father said. "Why else would she have said it?"

"Because of me," Lee admitted. "I told her that Paul still loved her. I told her *that day*. She felt responsible. She wanted to fix it."

"Lee," Pastor Bianchi said gently. "That doesn't make any sense."

"Of course it does," Lee persisted. "She knew

everyone would freak out. Never mind that God practiced infanticide. Never mind that He killed actual babies and not just little clumps of cells. She thought she could make some fake confession, and you would all be disgusted, and it would make Paul love me instead. Like that would work."

"You didn't even come into the sanctuary yesterday," Mrs. Bianchi said. "Everyone wanted to see you."

Yesterday, after Mrs. Bianchi left, Paul's parents had picked Lee up in their oversized car, just as the pastor's wife had said they would. Mr. and Mrs. Esposito had sat in the front seat, not speaking to her, and as Paul's mother played a cassette of church music very loudly through the back speakers, Lee recalled various pastors' descriptions of demon possession and how, when a possessed person heard the Lord's name, all the demons within him would come screaming to the surface. Once at church, Lee took Justine downstairs to the nursery where she remained for the entire five-hour service, holding Justine, who'd obligingly fallen asleep. No one came to fetch her and she didn't know whether she felt disappointed or relieved. Now, looking at Mrs. Bianchi's gentle, gray eyes, Lee felt the darkness enclose her. "No one wanted to see me," she said.

"Stop with that," Paul's father scolded. "Pastor Lou and Kathleen are being good to you. You can't talk to them like that."

"It's all right, Eddie," Pastor Bianchi said. "It's a hard time."

Paul's father stood and put on his hat. "I'll walk you to your car, Pastor."

"No need, Eddie." The pastor laid a hand on Paul's father's arm. "We'll take the baby. You stay with Lee."

Mrs. Bianchi lifted Justine, who looked heavy and large straddling Mrs. Bianchi's waist, her face pointing away. Lee momentarily wanted to take Justine from Mrs. Bianchi, to wrap her arms around her, the child's vertebrae against her forearms. But she only nodded when Mrs. Bianchi said, "I'll bring her over after you're home."

When the pastor's wife turned to leave, Lee could finally meet her daughter's eyes. She knew she should smile at her or wink or wave, but her own body felt heavy and slow, and she could only watch as the pastor's wife followed the pastor out of the store, carrying Justine.

After they were gone, Paul's father looked at Lee as though nothing could be more terrible than spending time alone with her, but his voice was kind when he asked, "Do you know how to read music, Lee?"

"No."

"Well, why don't I show you? Sometimes if you play, it brings customers in."

They sat side by side on a piano bench and Paul's father propped open a song book entitled *E-Z Play for the Beginner,* which contained sheet music with labeled notes. The song was "The Alley Cat," and he said, "They played this at mine and Mary's 25th anniversary, remember?" Lee nodded but didn't remember. Paul's parents' anniversary had been held in the party room of a restaurant called Tommy's, the same party room Paul's parents had rented for her and Paul's wedding reception, just shortly afterward. They shouldn't have had a reception at all, Lee knew, as it was Lee's responsibility, as the bride, to pay for it, and she couldn't afford one. She'd even bought her dress at the Goodwill, and Rachel had altered it to make it look all right. ("Now Rachel, *she* can sew," Paul's mother had said, admiring the alterations.) But Paul's parents had been generous, offering them a choice between a reception and a honeymoon, but reminding them that a reception would be the better choice, as it was less selfish and weddings were really "more for the family than the couple." Paul had immediately cast his vote for the reception rather than the trip, and it was only later that Lee understood he'd probably chosen it because he hadn't wanted to spend a week traveling with her. He'd preferred, Lee thought, to have a party that included Rachel, who wore a dress she'd made herself, a dress she'd worn at her own wedding. Rachel, who could sew. Rachel, the beautiful bride.

"So it goes like this," Paul's father said, his right hand on the piano keys. "You see that note that says C. Well, here's the C right here. That's called Middle C and it just goes up alphabetically through G then starts over again at A."

Lee pried her attention away from the past and nodded. "I've heard of Middle C," she said.

"It's famous," Paul's father agreed, and despite herself, Lee almost smiled to hear the "fame" of a piano key.

"OK, now pay attention to my right hand," Paul's father instructed. "Try to watch it and the sheet music at the same time, can you?" He played slowly, and Lee was able to watch his hand and the music at the same time. The piano belted out a slow version of the cheery, slinky, sexy melody of "The Alley Cat" and Lee remembered the tune. She could even picture Mr. and Mrs. Esposito dancing to it at their anniversary. Had Rachel been at that party? She couldn't remember. But Paul had danced quite memorably with Rachel at his and Lee's own wedding, during the traditional game in which the guests pay a dollar to dance with either the bride or groom. Alan had danced chastely with Lee while Rachel had danced with Paul, her arms wrapped tightly around him, Paul's mother on the sidelines, taking photographs. In her wedding dress, with flowers in her hair, Rachel had looked awfully bridal. And Paul, Lee thought now, had gazed more lovingly at Rachel than he had at Lee in any of the photographs in which she had managed to appear.

"Now tell me when I hit a wrong note," Paul's father said. "Ready?"

Rachel and Paul continued to dance in Lee's imagination while, at the piano, the tune faltered obviously. "That should have been an F," Lee told Paul's father.

"Good," he said.

"How about now?" He played another few notes.

"That should have been an A," she said.

"Good! Are you watching the sheet music?"

"No," Lee apologized. She looked at it hastily but had completely lost her place. Paul's father gave her an inquisitive look. "You play it," he said.

"I can't."

"Sure you can. You've got the notes right there." He patted her roughly on the head. "Just give it a try. A squirrel could do it."

She placed her right thumb on "famous" Middle C and began. Again, she saw Paul and Rachel dancing together. Rachel swung her hips from side to side and Paul closed his eyes in delight. She closed her eyes and kept playing. She could join them this way, she told herself, be part of them. Then she remembered the sheet music. Without it, she had played perfectly, but as soon as she tried to read those fat, black notes on the page, her hand faltered.

Paul's father walked away from her and sat at another piano in the back of the store. Lee didn't know whether to keep playing. "I'm sorry," she said, stopping.

"Can you see my hands, Lee?" Paul's father asked.

She stood up, trying to look. "No." She started to walk toward him.

"Stay there," he said. "Where you can't see. I want to try something." He played a note; Lee recognized it as an A. "What note is this?"

"It's an A."

"How about this?" He played a D.

"It's a D."

"You can't see my hands?"

"No!"

"What do you know?" he said.

"What?"

"I'm going to play something," he said. "Just a few notes and I want you to play them back to me from over there." He played a few notes. They were sad notes, and Lee repeated them. Was he trying to tell her something? He played some other tunes: happier, sadder, sillier, and Lee repeated them all. Paul's father must think she's awfully stupid, Lee decided.

"You never played any kind of music, Lee?"

"No."

"Did anyone in your family play music?"

"Not that I know of." What kind of family did he think she'd been raised in? Certainly, he knew she hadn't sat around playing piano.

"What do you know?" he said again.

"You said a squirrel could do it," Lee reminded him.

"Not this," he answered. "This is something you're born with. Almost no one can do this."

But she didn't know what he meant until she heard him on the phone with Paul's mother, almost an hour later. "You want to hear something wild?" she heard him say. "The daughter-in-law's got perfect pitch."

"What's perfect pitch?" she asked.

But he didn't answer directly. Instead, he said, "You could do something with music, you know. You'd pick it up like that. Paulie, well, he never took to it, but with what you've got, I'd say, in a year, you could be good enough to play for the church."

She integrated this new fact into what she knew about herself. She imagined being positioned at the front of the church, playing piano or otherwise performing with those Pastor Bianchi referred to as "the music ministry." But Paul and Rachel would watch from the sanctuary, probably smirking sidelong at one another whenever Lee made a mistake. "I couldn't," Lee told Mr. Esposito. She cast about for an explanation. "I'm too shy."

"That's too bad," Paul's father said. "It might make a difference for you and Paulie."

"What do you mean?"

Paul's father blinked rapidly then answered, "It's just it could be good for you and Paulie to get involved in the church more. When he gets back." His voice trailed away.

"If," said Lee.

So that's what this whole game was about, she thought. Distraction. She probably didn't have perfect pitch at all.

"Lee," Paul's father said. "Lee, there's a customer."

It was true. An elderly woman stood at the front end of the store, gazing intently at the self-playing organ. Lee approached, weighed down with sadness, her throat dry. "Can I help you?" she offered. Her voice sounded underconfident, and she expected the woman to walk away in disgust.

"What?" Clearly, she was nearly deaf. "How does it do this?"

"Play by itself?" Lee asked. "There's a computer chip inside." She wasn't sure she was right, but when she glanced back at Paul's father, he nodded vigorously.

"A what?" the woman asked.

"A computer chip," Lee repeated, louder.

"Computer?" she asked and Lee nodded, paralyzed. She knew she needed to keep the sale going but couldn't understand how. Why in the world would anyone sell an organ to a deaf woman? The woman looked at her and they shared an aching pause. Then Paul's father came bounding forward, smiling Paul's smile.

"I'm Eddie," he said, extending a hand and completely at ease.

"Vicky Martucci," she replied, seemingly able to hear just fine.

"Do you want to see what else it can do, Mrs. Martucci?" Paul's father asked. And he showed her all the buttons on the organ, paying particular attention to the one that made it sound like an old-fashioned player piano. "Just like the old days," he said, "only you don't have to load those rolls of paper because it's computerized, see?"

By the time Mrs. Martucci was ready to purchase the organ, she'd talked about her grandchildren, how much she enjoyed living in the retirement village, and her husband, who was at home with pleurisy.

"Pleurisy," Paul's father repeated, "that's tough."

"Ahh," Mrs. Martucci replied with asperity. "He's always got some damned thing or other," and she and Paul's father shared a small, comfortable laugh.

In the end, Mrs. Martucci paid for the organ in full on her Master Card and Paul's father scheduled a delivery for the next evening. The whole sale, start to finish, took no longer than ten minutes. Mrs. Martucci hugged Paul's father good-bye at the end. Lee waited for him to reprimand her, but he only finished writing up the receipt and said, "I'll put your name on this. That way you can get the commission."

Was it a test? "But I didn't do anything," she protested. "I wouldn't have even known what to do."

"Just be their friend," Paul's father replied. "That's why people buy that particular organ. They're looking for something besides the TV to keep them company."

"But she couldn't even hear it."

For a moment, he looked at her. "You know, you're a humble kid. Maybe even too humble. Selling's weird.

It's not about what people need. It's about making them feel good about buying things they don't need. But that's probably not your kind of thing, is it?"

"Not really," Lee answered. But she wished it was a skill she could cultivate, that she could persuade Paul to feel good about choosing her, even though he needed Rachel. "But I want to help," she added. "If Paul comes back, I want to be able to help him."

"I don't like to see humble people get hurt," Paul's father persisted. "Go to that prayer meeting tonight." Then, seeming to have nothing further to say, he lowered his head and closed his eyes.

***

Pastor and Mrs. Bianchi lived close enough to Paul and Lee that it wasn't necessary to drive to their house, even though Paul's parents would have. Lee spent a long time dressing, though she wasn't sure why. Then she spent an equally long time planning what Justine would wear. She finally decided on almost matching dresses with floral prints, and she packed Justine's favorite stuffed puppies in a wicker picnic basket. Mr. Esposito's assessment of her as a "humble kid" had given Lee a more satisfying identity to try on than "undeserving, abandoned wife."

She carried Justine as she walked. She wore straw colored sandals; Justine's sandals were white. They looked humble, Lee told herself, humble kids out for a walk in the sunlight of a late summer evening. Would Paul's father call him, wherever he and Rachel had gone, and say, "You made a mistake, Paulie. Come back. Lee's a humble kid." Would it be enough? She looked down at her bare toes protruding from her straw-colored sandals, and her bravado vanished. The dress she wore was stupid and garish, and her legs were too skinny to be this exposed. Humble wouldn't work after all, she decided. The description was as false as the allegation of her perfect pitch. "Do you want to go home instead of to the Bianchis'?" she asked Justine.

"Can we play Puppy?"

"Sure. But no stories of their lives, OK?"

No one phoned to ask why she hadn't come to the meeting. Lee went through the motions of an evening; she played with Justine, bathed her, and read to her before bedtime. Justine chose a book about a jealous dog who tries to win back his owner's love by building an enormous plaster egg and hatching from it.

"This story makes me think of your daddy," Lee told Justine.

"Daddy's a puppy!" Justine laughed. Then, quietly,

seriously, she asked, "Where's Daddy?"

"On a trip," Lee answered, trying to smile. "With Auntie Rachel."

"He comes home yesterday?" Justine asked. Then, she corrected herself. "Tomorrow?"

Lee kissed her daughter's forehead. "Mommy's here," she said. And she took the stuffed dogs from the wicker basket one by one, making each kiss Justine on the cheek.

Afterward, Lee paced from room to quiet room, turning lights on and off, picking up toys, wondering how she would ever fill the empty space. She could buy one of those self-playing organs, she told herself wryly. But, she wouldn't be able to keep the house, she reminded herself. If Paul *didn't* come home, Paul's parents wouldn't want her to work in the store anymore, and waitressing would never pay the bills. And if Paul came home with Rachel, everyone would want them to live here. With Justine.

When the doorbell rang, she expected to find Paul and Rachel, poised to evict her. Upon opening the door, Lee needed a few moments to identify her callers as Amy Rotolo's parents, followed closely by Alan.

"Let us in," Mrs. Rotolo commanded. "We're here to pray."

Mrs. Rotolo, as always, wore enough perfume for

the smell of synthetic flowers to fill the entire first floor of Lee's house. She passed Lee without smiling and said, "Make some tea, would you?" while Mr. Rotolo said nothing. Alan patted Lee's shoulder and said, "Praise the Lord, Sister."

Overpowered with sympathy for Rachel, Lee wanted to ask, "For what?"

She filled the kettle.

"You don't have to do all that," Mrs. Rotolo said. "The microwave is fine."

"It's just a kettle," Lee answered.

"It's slow." She scowled. Then, seeming to recover from her disappointment in Lee's chosen method of boiling water, said, "Your mother-in-law is in a right state about you, I don't mind telling you."

"She sent you guys?" Lee caught a shadowy glimpse of Mr. Rotolo in the living room, staring at framed photographs. One of them, Lee realized, showed Paul, Rachel, and Amy Rotolo as children.

Mrs. Rotolo gestured over one shoulder with her thumb, indicating Alan. "She sent *him*, but I thought Vic and I should come too. It's improper, given the circumstances, for you and Alan to be alone in your house at night."

Lee nearly laughed aloud. She had never felt less seductive, nor, indeed, had she ever met anyone less suited for seduction than Alan. "My life is a lot more interesting in your imagination," she said.

"Temptation is not interesting," Mrs. Rotolo answered.

"Look," Alan said. "I know how you feel."

"About what?"

The kettle whistled.

"About everything with Rachel and Paul. That's why I'm here."

"I'm sorry," Lee said, handing the cup to Mrs. Rotolo. "I haven't got the strength or energy to talk about that right now."

"The joy of the Lord can be your strength," Alan said, which prompted Mrs. Rotolo to begin singing a song inspired by that particular scripture. Mrs. Rotolo sang when she felt uncomfortable; Amy had once told Lee that.

"The Lord is going to forgive them," Alan continued, shouting slightly over Mrs. Rotolo's song. "It's like I said to Rachel when she called. It's between them and the Lord and we'll still be here when they're right with God."

"Hallelujah," Mrs. Rotolo said.

Lee felt light-headed. "Rachel called you?"

"Yes," Alan answered, glancing at Mrs. Rotolo, as though for direction. "Just once."

"Where are they? Are they together?"

"She didn't say that."

"Really?"

"Just that they're both safe." Alan and Mrs. Rotolo exchanged a significant look. "We thought they'd gone to Amy's, but the Lord tells me they aren't there," Alan said.

"They aren't." Lee didn't need the Lord to tell her this. "Amy likes me. She wouldn't let them stay there. Separately, maybe, but not together."

"Amy would do anything that she thought might hurt her father and me," Mrs. Rotolo answered.

"Hurt *you*?" Lee asked.

"Let's pray," Mrs. Rotolo said. Then she called, "Vic! Come in here. We're praying."

They sat around the kitchen table; the electric overhead light glowed against the polished wood. Lee regarded the splotch of color with amazement. As a child, when she'd lived in so many places, never knowing what would come next nor how long she would be permitted to stay anywhere, she would never have believed this was possible. *My house,* she told herself again, *my husband; my clean, electric light.* But again her claims evaporated. *Of course they're safe. I'm the one who isn't safe.*

"Thank You, Lord Jesus," Alan said, "for the great

work of healing You're doing in our lives. Thank You, Lord Jesus, that whenever two or more are gathered in Your name, You are in our midst." He spoke in Tongues then, the Rotolos chiming in with their own brands of nonsense syllables.

This went on a long time. Even if God were listening, Lee thought, wouldn't He attend to the world's more pressing problems instead? Amy Rotolo had once told her, "You're too insecure for salvation," and Lee had been stunned by Amy's absolute accuracy.

"The Lord is telling me something," Alan interjected once his and the Rotolos' prayers had tapered into sleepy silence. "Lee, I need to ask you about something that the Lord just laid on my heart."

"Yes?"

"Are you angry with the Lord, Lee?"

"What?"

"I just felt the Lord prodding me in that direction," Alan said, "and I wondered if you were angry with Him. I saw you standing alone, shaking your fist at Him."

"Hallelujah," Mrs. Rotolo said.

"You saw me?"

"With my prophetic eye," Alan answered earnestly. "You were standing alone and you were younger, almost a little girl, and you were angry with God."

"What happened when you were younger, Lee?" Mr. Rotolo asked.

Lee knew the answer that would provide a clean package of cause and effect. She could tell them about being small and left alone by her mother, without food or electricity, for days. She could tell them that she prayed, first to God, then to every deity she'd ever heard of, even Satan, but that no one came. She could tell them how her mother died soon afterward and how she was shunted from place to place, trying each time to memorize enough Bible verses and to complete enough chores to bribe her new hosts into becoming her family. She could tell them she'd never stopped this particular behavior, and that, even after a lifetime of attempts, she'd never learned to do it right.

Amy's parents looked at her, waiting. "I'm not angry at God," she said. "Everyone has a hard childhood."

"Not everyone," Mrs. Rotolo answered.

Lee knew she meant Amy, who had been spoiled with all sorts of expensive things. "I hate to sound like a poor little rich girl," Amy had once said to Lee. "I really hate it."

"They never loved you," Lee had answered. "They adored the idea of being parents, maybe, but they never loved *you*."

"That's exactly right," Amy had said gratefully.

"I'm not angry at God," Lee repeated.

"How old were you when your mother died?" Mrs. Rotolo asked.

"Quite young," Lee answered. Then, as though she couldn't remember, added, "You know, four or five."

Mrs. Rotolo clicked her tongue against her teeth.

"But it wouldn't have mattered if she hadn't," Lee said. "She didn't love me. That's what matters. You can make a show of loving someone. You can buy them all kinds of things or let them live in your big house, but it's always obvious when it's not real."

"You think Paul doesn't love you?" Mrs. Rotolo asked, but Mr. Rotolo had drawn a sharp breath and Lee knew he, at least, understood she wasn't talking only of Paul.

"I know he doesn't," Lee said. "He told me the night of the prayer meeting. He loves Rachel, not me."

"The Lord commands us to love our wives," Alan said. "You gave me that scripture."

"Of course he loves you," Mrs. Rotolo echoed. "You're his wife."

***

Lee made it, somehow, through two more days at the store while the Bianchis babysat Justine. Both days, after retrieving Justine from the pastor's house, Lee hurried to the mailbox, hoping to see Paul's handwriting. No letter came. Nor did he phone. What were he and Rachel doing? Perhaps, even now, they were returning to Riverview together. On Tuesday evening, Lee began to pack. She wouldn't take anything Paul or her in-laws had given her, she decided, but she'd take every photograph of Justine in the house.

On Wednesday night, Lee had no excuse to miss church. This time, she did not dress in clothes that complemented her daughter's. Briefly, she toyed with the idea of wearing red, just to show she was aware of the controversy she inhabited, but instead chose to wear gray. Safe, quiet, penitent gray. I am sorry, her dress would imply, for occupying a life that should not have been mine. I am sorry for my usurpations and improprieties. I am sorry for the space I take up and the gossip you've had to hear about me. I am sorry I am not Rachel.

Paul's parents arrived in their large car, and Lee was surprised that her mother-in-law had also chosen to wear gray. Her face looked different: older, more taut and careworn, and Lee felt a momentary, unexpected pang of kinship. "Give Grandma a kiss," she told Justine, and Justine held her stuffed dog to

Paul's mother's cheek. Lee watched Paul's mother struggling to smile. *Don't cry,* she pleaded silently. *Please, Mrs. Esposito; she'll think she's done something wrong if you cry.* Then she wondered if she should be thinking something else.

Perhaps Justine felt confused, too. She looked at Lee, as though for reassurance, held up her cloth puppy, and asked, "Now can you tell Roscoe the story of his life?"

"Of course," Lee answered. "After church."

Lee settled Justine into the backseat and sat beside her. Paul's mother pivoted, revealing red eyes. What story could accommodate Paul and his family, too? What if she told the story of everything that had happened since the prayer meeting? What if the stuffed dog, Roscoe, was an insecure virgin bride, daughter of a dead mother, wife of a husband who loved someone else? But as she ran silently through the beginning of that story, she surprised herself by finding it boring.

Abortion was a boring thing to make a fuss about, she decided. Fanaticism was boring. It was boring to be the insecure wife of a small time New Jersey salesman. It was boring to be jealous of her husband's high school sweetheart; it was boring to be a virgin bride; it was boring to have a dead mother; it was boring to feel rejected; it was boring to feel unloved. Life and its feelings exist in other names, she told herself, not the names you see on television, not the names you hear people say. I'm not really jealous, she told herself. I just think I'm jealous because I've seen this story before. I've seen the story of my childhood and how it's supposed to affect me. I've seen stories about religious fanatics and mothers and children, and I've believed the corresponding elements of my life should fit into the forms I've already seen. Even worse, everyone else thinks the same way. This isn't how any of us would really act. My mother's hatred, my jealousy, Paul's flight, and his mother's melodrama are all straight from television. Boring television.

She leaned against the cool upholstery of Paul's parents' car. Immediately lulled by the drive, Justine had fallen asleep, holding Roscoe, the stuffed dog, its plastic nose and eyes pointed toward Lee, as though awaiting the story she'd promised. How many times had Lee told these stories, elaborately describing toys' experiences of being lost beneath the bed or being thrown in the washing machine as emblematic moments of mortal peril, making Justine giggle until she lost her breath? She patted Roscoe's cloth head. These last few days of grief and despair were boring, too, she thought. And she remembered the stain made by the spilled Coke during the second day of Paul's absence. It had been shaped something like Alaska. That stain, she decided, was interesting. It had so many possible interpretations, but none fit exactly; it existed only in the space beyond. That's me, too, she thought. That's everyone.

Lee held Justine's wrist, feeling the child's impossibly resilient skin against her palm. Justine briefly roused, opened her eyes halfway, looked for Lee, found her, and, quite clearly comforted, closed her eyes again, sleepily smiling to herself. Paul was wrong, Lee thought, to say that love guaranteed nothing. At the very least, it guaranteed that her daughter could grow up in a world completely different from the one Lee herself had always known, a world that, if Lee could build it and hold onto it, was bigger than Paul and his parents and the church, a world that existed in the space beyond.

Anything could happen next: Paul could come back or not. He could stay with Rachel or not. Lee could lose the house, lose the church, lose Paul. Anything could happen. But no matter what that entailed, she would not lose her daughter. She would make sure of that.

The car stopped. They had arrived at church. Lee woke her daughter and smiled at her mother-in-law, not caring what her mother-in-law would think. She felt buoyant. *This* was salvation, she told herself, and she took Justine's hand.

Trained Children

The Oregon pub smelled of fried food and perfume ("ylang ylang" Rachel called it) and Paul sat beside Rachel at the bar, watching a guitarist play folk songs on a makeshift stage. "Freedom," the guitarist sang, "plutonium."

Paul had never, he realized, been inside a pub. He thought of his mother's welling eyes and his father's stern disapproval. So many times, he'd been told that demons lived in places like this. When he was a teenager listening to Pastor Bianchi's litany of demon-infested activities, Paul had imagined demons to be a bit like germs, sitting on every surface, waiting to attach to whatever touched them.

After driving nearly non-stop for three days with no plan beyond arriving at Amy's, they'd practically been turned away at the door. Afterward, Rachel had asked, "Have you ever gotten drunk?"

So, they drank. With almost frightening authority, Rachel had ordered rum and cokes for each of them. "I loved these in college," she said.

"You went to a Christian college!"

"It wasn't a monastery." She shrugged. "I mean, I took the Pledge like everyone else, but we still went into town."

Paul hadn't been raised to drink. Sin, he thought as he sipped. He couldn't tell if he liked the taste or not. But he kept drinking. At this point, what was one more sin?

All week, before leaving with Rachel, the days had passed, gauzy and unreal, with Paul moving through them, waiting, it seemed, until everyone could forget the need to shame him.

When his parents' friends saw him, they said, "Hallelujah" in greeting before looking away, as though he carried some contagious disease. How had his parents spoken to so many people so quickly? And what had they said? That he'd had pre-marital sex as a teenager? That he'd somehow, unwittingly colluded in a secret abortion? To Paul, it all seemed ludicrous, but how could it be when, to everyone else he knew, it all made perfect sense? All his life, Paul had heard Pastor Lou's fervent pulpit declaration, "Be in the world, not *of* the world. The world thinks we're crazy!" And while the congregation answered with praises and amens, Paul often thought he was of neither the church nor the world.

Meanwhile, his mother made sure to ask

deliberately hurtful questions like, "Do you think it might have been a boy?"

For a day or two, he had tried to argue, but although his parents claimed to believe he hadn't known about the abortion, they wouldn't believe the abortion itself hadn't happened.

"And *you* put her in that position," his mother said. "You're every bit as much to blame. You should have married her if you wanted to sleep with her. You don't just take that from a girl and then break up."

And because his parents believed it was true, it seemed to Paul that whether Rachel had lied was immaterial. Fiction or not, "the baby" existed; moreover, its existence had become more important, in his parents' eyes at least, than Justine's or even his own.

Lee also seemed in no rush to stop shaming him. She slept on the living room couch at night. At dinnertime, she cooked and served dinner for him and Justine then stood to the side and watched them eat. Afterward, she cleaned the dishes as though Paul were her employer. After Justine went to bed, Lee mentioned Rachel and started another brutal fight. How strange and stupid, Paul sometimes thought, that one prayer meeting could have turned his whole life into a catastrophe.

Then, just three evenings ago, after putting Justine to bed, Lee came into the living room holding a large collection of photographs of Rachel, unearthed from somewhere. "She's always been so beautiful," Lee said, her voice crazily, strenuously calm as she arranged the photographs on the living room carpet. "She looks like a movie star."

"What are you doing?" He sat on the couch, frozen with dread.

"This is nice," Lee said, holding Paul and Rachel's high school prom picture.

"Lee."

"She came home this morning, you know. Your mother called. She asked me if you knew." Her voice had risen slightly. Something's going to break, Paul thought.

"Lee."

"You should go," she continued, "while Justine's asleep. I don't want her to watch you leave."

"Lee," he repeated. "Put the pictures away."

Without warning, she was on her feet and charging at him, her fists raised. "Go!" He kept absolutely still while she screamed, pushed him, slammed into him with her fists, scratched his face with her fingernails. "Get out of here! Go be with her. It's what you want. Just go!"

How long this went on, he couldn't guess. He watched her fists move toward him and then away and then toward him again. Something in her expression reminded him of the welfare families his parents had driven to church on long ago Sundays when Paul was young. He had always sat against his parents' legs in the front seat of their squat AMC Gremlin as they'd driven down the wide highway, past the tamely settled parts of town and into the frayed outskirts where rotting motels stood forebodingly. Always, a mother and her children had waited on a rickety balcony outside one of the motel rooms and they'd clamored into his parents' backseat. The families had always smelled surprisingly, abundantly clean and powdered, and Paul's father had cast uncertain, smiling glances backward at them through the rearview mirror. At church, the welfare families had always sat far away from Paul's family, and intermittently through the long services, Paul had caught their eyes, trying to determine whether he imagined the contempt he thought he saw in their meeting gazes. Now, looking at his wife, he decided that it *was* contempt he'd seen after all; it had always been contempt.

"You're so middle class," Lee would have said if he'd told her. "The middle class always blames the poor."

Instead, he caught one of her hands in his and asked, "What's wrong with you?"

"I said you should go." She wrenched free from his grip. On hands and knees, she crawled around, picking up the photographs she'd inadvertently scattered when she'd attacked him. When she'd collected them, she threw the whole messy stack at his head. "Go."

"This is crazy."

"Go," she said again. "Bye."

He didn't know what to do. He picked up the pictures, his wallet, and his keys, and decided to walk awhile, to give her time to cool off. And then? She had seemed so certain of him when they'd met. She'd bought him presents she couldn't afford—watches and cashmere scarves and any book or cassette tape he'd ever mentioned. When he'd told her that he didn't love her, she'd said that was all right. She'd said she would work to earn his love. "It's my way," she'd said. "It's what I've always done." And when he'd tried, early on, to create some distance between them, she'd gripped him even more tightly, finally giving him the ultimatum, "I'm done dating you. I'll get married if that's what you want, but I won't date you anymore." And it had sounded like an order, and his parents had raised him to take orders, so Paul had obeyed.

He walked many blocks until he reached

Riverview's main arterial then walked the arterial for a long time, finally stopping when he could see the headlights of highway traffic in the distance. It had gotten very late. He stood beneath a streetlight, near a sewer grate, kicked the curb, and idly paged through the old pictures. At so many points in his life, it seemed, rebellion would have made sense. But he'd merely said yes to orders. His father wanted him to manage one of the stores. His mother wanted him to buy his parents' old house. And he'd obeyed, again and again. Only Lee was off the mark. Paul's parents had always expected Paul to marry Rachel, but as she'd married Alan, it wasn't as if Paul could have married her, too. After Lee gave her ultimatum, Paul even thought his parents might accept her—a member of their church, Rachel's friend—as a happy compromise, a forgivably near miss. But, at their wedding, Paul's father had read the entire text of Proverbs 31, lingering especially on sections detailing how ceaselessly a virtuous woman must work to please her husband. Once he'd finished, his mother had segued into the Apostle Paul's letter to the Ephesians, declaring, "Wives submit yourselves unto your own husbands as unto the Lord. For the husband is the head of the wife." About six months after the wedding, though, when he and Lee, just a few months along, still went to bed at the same time, before their house smelled of talcum powder and apple juice, Paul had once caught his father standing in the doorway of his and Lee's bedroom. He saw Paul, nodded toward their dark green comforter, and wistfully said, "You guys have such a pretty bed." And Paul had remembered a long ago night when he'd woken to the sound of his mother crying. It went on a long time before Paul recognized it as laughter, a high-pitched laughter that seemed incongruous with everything he knew about his mother's voice. Then the laughter stopped and his mother's voice regained familiarity when she said, "Eddie, stop it. Get a prostitute if you want that." The next morning, over breakfast, Paul had felt very shy and sorry for his father.

He paged through the photos until he found one of him and Rachel dancing at his and Lee's wedding. He'd never had the faintest idea what he was doing, he thought, and he considered throwing all the pictures into the gutter.

"Looking for sewer rats?" Rachel had spotted him under the light and had driven alongside him as though someone had told her exactly where he'd be standing.

"Alligators," he answered, startled by her presence and then further surprised he was able to do something as normal as making a joke.

"What are you doing here?"

"What are *you* doing?"

"Are you bleeding?" With her chin, she indicated the passenger side door. "Get in."

He obeyed, not realizing quickly enough that the photos remained in his hand.

"Are those pictures of me?" she asked, glancing at them before the car's dome light extinguished.

He knew he should explain but only answered, "Yes."

"What do you know?" she said. And it seemed, as she turned onto the highway and he understood she was running away and taking him with her, that he did love Rachel, that she was a kind of home he'd known long ago and had missed ever since. But nearly three days of driving had passed, and sitting beside Rachel in the pub, he didn't know how he felt about anything.

They'd driven in shifts, stopping for gas or food, barely speaking. New Jersey had flown past before Paul could even begin to contemplate that he'd left; then came the arduously dull Pennsylvania Turnpike which led, heavily, into Ohio.

He didn't ask Rachel about their destination. The map on the dashboard told it with its highlighted route from New Jersey to Oregon. He hadn't brought extra clothes and had only eighty dollars in his wallet. Rachel, seemingly, had much more. "It's everything I ever made selling my art at church," she told him. "A few hundred bucks every Christmas Bazaar, a couple hundred every summer fair. Alan wouldn't touch it, so I just kept it. I just kept the cash in this weird ceramic kettle me and Alan got as a wedding present. I guess I always thought I might need it someday." And Paul understood he'd been a last minute addition, an impulse. What did his agreement to come along actually mean? What did he owe Rachel? When he wasn't driving, he often slept. Upon waking, he thought of criminals on television crime dramas; they always slept in their holding cells when first caught. Other times, he thought the word "refugee." At one point, Rachel asked, "Do you want to call Lee?"

"Do *you* want to call Alan?" he answered, almost angrily.

"Why did you marry her?" Rachel asked.

"Why did you marry Alan?"

"I asked first."

"You asked first?" Paul shook his head. "You got married first."

"Yeah," Rachel agreed. "Yeah, I guess I did."

After more than twenty-four hours, they'd nearly reached Nebraska, and Paul had begun to panic. They'd driven past signs announcing cities Paul had heard of his whole life but had never seen: Chicago, Cleveland, Des Moines. They'd driven through nighttime hours of flat, dark landscapes with nothing to watch except headlights reflecting off green highway signs. They'd driven through a day of heat and aching knees and hunger. Finally, it was night again and he and Rachel were sitting on the hood of the car, eating gas station cheeseburgers.

I'm a runaway, he thought. Like a little boy. A man wouldn't have left his wife and child to drive across the country with a former girlfriend who claimed to have aborted his child. A man wouldn't have betrayed his parents, his parents' friends, his parents' church. And what would he and Rachel do at Amy's house? He remembered those endless church services of his youth during which he, Rachel, and Amy had knelt at the altar, the pastor laying hands on them, to cast out their spirits. Once, the pastor told Paul that he'd seen literal demons flying from Paul's head. Obviously not, Paul thought as they finished their burgers, filled the gas tank, and continued to drive. If demons exist, I've still got them. He almost asked Rachel to turn back, but when it came time to form the words, it would have been easier to jump off a building.

There was no fixing this, he thought.

The next day, partway through Wyoming, the landscape changed. The plains had suddenly given way to spectacular buttes and hills and, finally, the Rocky Mountains, the likes of which he'd never imagined. New Jersey had its nearby mountain ranges: the Catskills in New York and the Poconos in Pennsylvania. As a kid, he'd been taken to both for family vacations. He and his parents had visited churches and amusement parks and wax museums in the hillside tourist towns. But those weren't mountains at all when compared to what he saw here.

"People actually live here," Paul said. "They just live around this all the time."

"They're used to it. It's like the ocean is to us," Rachel said. "No big deal."

"I'd never get used to it." He wanted to see everything. Dusk settled as they were driving down Highway 84, which had taken them into Oregon at last, and which had just brought them alongside a tremendous canyon he'd never expected, that he'd never even heard of existing. It was simply unbelievable, long and deep, rimmed by mountains and lit pink and orange by the setting sun. "Are we going the right way?" he asked Rachel, stunned.

"I think so," she answered, looking through the window. "What is it?"

"I don't know." There looked to be water at the very bottom, reflecting the sunset and the canyon walls. "We're in the West," he said, realizing this for the first time. "That's why the sunset's so crazy."

"Maybe they don't have sunrise services on Easter out here," Rachel said. "Remember, it was like a whole day of church before we could get our candy? And how we had to write our sins on those little pieces of paper and nail them to that cross on the altar?"

Nearby signs announced a town called The Dalles. "Let's stop and look before it gets dark," Paul said. How could this exist and not be known around the world?

"I want to get there." Rachel pointed to a roadside sign that counted down miles to other Oregon towns. Amy's was listed at the very bottom.

They kept driving. Lee would have stopped, he thought almost sulkily. Lee—who'd never been taken anywhere as a child—appreciated just about everything. She even bundled up to brave the cold, desolate Atlantic Ocean beaches in the middle of winter, just because she missed the way the ocean smelled. "You're a cheap date, Lee," Paul's father had teased her once. "Yes," she'd agreed, a little sadly, perhaps. "I suppose I am."

The dark came, ultimately extinguishing Paul's

view of the canyon and whatever lay beyond it. They exited one highway and merged with another. 90 miles. Then 60. At 35 miles to go, they bought gas for what Paul knew would be the last time. It was late, just after midnight. Again, he wished they had stopped at the canyon, had slept in the car for the night, and had woken to see it lit by sunrise. What did sunrise look like in the West? Those Easter services had never bothered him, actually. He had always liked to see all the mothers dressed up in their hats and fancy shoes, walking into the building under the new sun.

"I'll drive the rest of the way," Rachel offered, glancing at a local map she'd evidently just bought at the gas station.

"It's kind of late," Paul said.

"I called her the day I got back. She said I could come anytime."

He hadn't known what to expect of Amy's house, having never been in a lesbian household before, and could only imagine hand-drawn scenes of demons and orgies from scare-tactic comic book tracts sometimes distributed at church. As kids, he, Rachel, and Amy had collected those tracts, one of which, he remembered, was entitled "The Gay Blade." Its cover pictured a cartoon man with a handlebar moustache and a lascivious grin. A fat cartoon demon stood proudly behind him. At the time, Paul couldn't fathom what any of it meant. But Amy's house, it transpired, had no telltale cartoon demons. The only thing it suggested, in fact, was that Amy had no money at all.

"Is this right?" Paul asked. The house, or half-house more accurately, occupied the left-hand side of a side-by-side duplex. From the road, it looked narrower than the breadth of his outstretched arms. A porch light illuminated the front door's warped, chipped wood. The house had no front window. It was too small to accommodate one.

"It's so tiny." Rachel checked the address she'd written on the map.

"Isn't she a nurse?" Paul asked. "I thought nurses did pretty well."

Rachel shook her head. "Maybe rents are really expensive here or something." She got out of the car and Paul followed. The other half of the side-by-side was quite obviously vacant. The gutted body of an old Volkswagen sat in front of it, detritus, perhaps, of a previous tenant. They made their way across Amy's overgrown front yard—no clear path existed—to the front steps, which led to a lopsided firetrap of a porch. The cool, quiet air smelled of a pulp mill. One must be nearby, Paul thought.

Next to the front door, above the doorbell, hung

a small wooden plaque. Amy's parents had one, too, in the exact spot, which bore the scripture, "As for me and my house, we will serve the Lord." He found it surprising that Amy would carry that tradition forward, but as his eyes adjusted to the porch light, he saw this plaque carried a different message: "And this above all: To thine own self be true."

"That isn't the Bible, is it?" Paul asked Rachel.

"Definitely not," Rachel said, reading it. "I think it's Shakespeare."

"What if they're sleeping?" he asked.

But Rachel knocked. The sound echoed through the quiet night, disturbing some neighborhood dogs, who howled.

"Let's go," Paul said. "It's too late."

But the front door opened, revealing a woman who wasn't Amy. Paul was astounded by how pretty she looked, half-asleep, in the porch light.

"Theresa?" Rachel asked.

"Yes." She blinked at them, evidently waking.

"Is that Amy's…um…?" Paul whispered to Rachel.

"Yes," Theresa answered. "I'm her 'um.'" Even knowing it was stupid, he'd expected someone different—a woman who looked like a man, perhaps with slim hips and a vague moustache. "You're from that church, right?" Theresa asked. "That crazy church?"

Rachel apparently thought "that crazy church" couldn't possibly refer to their own. "No," she said. "We're her old friends. From Riverview. I'm Rachel. This is Paul. Amy invited me."

"Amy's not here." Behind Theresa, Paul could see the outlines of a bed and a table. "She works nights. I work days."

"We're sorry," Paul said. They lived in a one-room house. It felt necessary to apologize. "We're sorry we woke you."

"We were invited," Rachel repeated. "Or at least I was. But she'd be OK with Paul too. We've both known her, like, forever?"

"Of course she invited you," Theresa answered. "Amy wants that crazy church to chase her right now."

"Chase her?" Rachel asked.

Theresa sighed. "She was basically disowned last week."

"Rachel," Paul said. "Let's come back tomorrow."

"But see, I've talked to her since then," Rachel told Theresa. "I had a bad week, too. She said I could come anytime."

"I get up at five," Theresa said. "We're health aides, me and Amy. It's a very physical job, hard to do on no sleep."

"We're sorry," Paul said again. "Go back to bed.

We'll call her tomorrow."

Theresa began to close the door, but Rachel said, "Wait."

"Rachel. Let's go."

"No, wait." She moved closer to the door. "Her parents think she's a nurse."

Theresa shrugged. "She's an adult. She doesn't have to tell them everything."

"But they have no idea."

"No idea about what?" Theresa asked. "That she's not a nurse? She will be when she's done with school."

"Go back to bed," Paul repeated. "This can wait."

"But listen," Rachel persisted. "When she said I could come, I thought that meant, that..." She gestured toward the house. "You know..."

"Oh." Theresa gave a harsh laugh. "Oh, you didn't realize that we're..." She shook her head. "What did you expect? We both had to start completely from scratch."

"I just thought..."

"Thought what?" She looked angry. "That we're out here running some grand sinners' resort? With amenities? And you could come here? Relax in a hot tub while you piss off all the right people and then go back all rested up, like you just had a vacation?"

"I didn't mean it like that," Rachel said. "Anyway, we *can't* go back."

But Theresa contradicted her. "Yes, you can. Of course you can. Amy's the only one who can't go back." From the recesses of the room came a baby's cry. "That's our nephew," Theresa said. "He's staying with us while my sister… Never mind. Anyway. He's up, thanks. I've gotta go."

"Your nephew?" Paul asked. "How are you managing?"

"Look," Theresa said. "I don't know what you're thinking about us, but Amy and I have a good life together, a happy life. When you go back, if anyone asks, be sure you tell them that."

It was afterward, in Amy's front yard, that Rachel had asked, "Have you ever gotten drunk?"

Now, Paul drank until the walls moved.

"It makes Alan's house look like a palace," Rachel said.

"But they're happy. She said they're happy."

"With three people living in one room?"

"She said they're fine," Paul said.

Rachel ordered more drinks. "She just always had so much."

Paul nodded.

They'd all been neighbors. His parents had bought the house next door to the Rotolos', and Rachel and her parents had lived around the block. As kids, the three of them rode bikes together. Amy's bike was always the shiniest and newest. The Rotolos still had their in-ground pool, and the three of them would play in Amy's backyard during the summers, her mom running in and out of the house with pitchers of horrible, minty iced tea Paul had never liked in all his years of being made to drink it. Amy had a fat, gold commemorative coin her father had received for donating money to the 700 Club, and they took turns throwing the coin into the deep end of the pool and then swimming down, ears popping, lungs tight, to retrieve it, careful always not to tear the pool liner, which, her father often reminded them, he would never forgive.

On summer evenings, when Paul, Rachel, and some other neighborhood kids played kickball in the street, they heard Amy practicing her singing or clarinet through the Rotolos' open windows. And, sometimes, Paul's own father would perform duets with Amy in church—Paul's father on piano, and Amy singing—on special occasions like Christmas Eve. In high school, Amy had leads in all the school plays, took gifted classes, and did gymnastics on the Varsity squad. She wore nice clothes and always had her parents in the front row, cheering for her. He wouldn't have predicted this future for her, either.

"I can't believe she's not even a nurse," Rachel continued.

"Well, she *will* be."

Rachel stirred her drink. "It's messed up, though. Her parents have so much money. If they knew how she was living."

"They'd say it was what she reaped," Paul said. "Honor your father and mother and all that. That's why she never told them." He remembered an argument he'd once witnessed between Amy and her mother. He was young enough that his feet didn't quite touch the floor as he sat at her parents' table. Or maybe that was a trick of memory because Amy, who was his age exactly, seemed so grown up. She'd stood, her fists on her hips, her red face yelling out names like "Buddha," "The Dalai Lama," and "Sartre," and her mother, positioned on the other side of the table, yelled the word "Hell!" after each of these names. Her mother, Paul remembered, was smiling. Maybe it was just a trick of memory, but he remembered her smiling more triumphantly with each articulation of Amy's heroes' burning fate. Later, standing on the manicured sod in front of the Rotolos' house, Amy had apologized to him. "You shouldn't have to witness my family's histrionics," she'd said. "Damn, I gotta get out of here."

"But how long was she supposed to honor them?" Rachel said now. "Even when she's an adult, she's supposed to live how they say or get cut off without a dime?"

Yes, Paul realized. Yes, that was exactly how it worked. Well into his adulthood, his mother, in the overly articulate, dramatic voice she reserved for scripture, had quoted at him, "Honor your father and your mother, for this is the first commandment with a promise." Then, staring at him, she'd say, "Nothing will go well for you if you disobey." So, year after year, he'd obeyed. And they'd rewarded his obedience by cementing his debt to them; for more than a year, they'd supplemented his income enough to keep the store running until Paul finally learned how to run it himself. They'd practically given him their old house. He hadn't asked for any of it, true, but he hadn't worked for any of it, either.

"Amy knew what she'd lose," he told Rachel. "It was worth it to her." Was it better to suffer through entrenchment or through absolute separation? Those were his and Amy's only options, Paul thought sadly.

Rachel shook her head. "I was always too scared. Even when my parents died and I could have done anything, I was too scared." She looked at him. "My mom loved Alan."

"*My* mom loved *you*," said Paul.

"Used to," Rachel agreed.

Paul drank the rest of his cocktail. Rachel had paid for it, and he couldn't guess how much it cost. He wasn't used to worrying about money. He hadn't ever thought about this part of leaving home. He'd never understood how easily one could wind up with nothing.

"I guess I'm not scared anymore," Rachel said.

"I guess," Paul agreed. His head felt heavy. Without thinking, he leaned it against Rachel's shoulder, just for relief from its weight, and kissed her neck. He hadn't meant for it to happen. Afterward, in a motel room, as he held her and she looked him full in the face as Lee never had, as she grabbed his back as though every minute of emptiness he'd ever known belonged to her, too, Paul felt as though the world had come right, that he'd finally found what he wanted and who he was, and that everything would make sense for the rest of his life. Drunkenly, he compared himself to a three-legged stool that had previously been missing a leg. In bed, Lee was all timid fingers and frightened eyes, and, these days, by the time she was done putting their daughter to bed—making her "go potty" for what seemed like hours, giving her a bath, reading to her, singing to her—neither of them had any energy left. Lee would go to bed long before the 10:00 news because Justine would awaken before sunrise. Sometimes, during the brief hours he and Lee had to themselves, Paul would initiate something. More often, they would simply sit and watch television. On one rare, recent occasion, when he'd reached for Lee in bed, he'd found a stuffed Pekinese beneath the covers. "No more of these," he'd said, throwing the toy across the room.

"They're not expensive or anything, you know." Lee had misunderstood his annoyance. "That one cost thirty cents at the Goodwill. And it's good for her imagination. The more she has, the more games she can make up with them."

He hadn't said anything. He'd only lain awake awhile, trying to remember the last time they'd even kissed on the lips.

Now, Rachel rested her head on his chest and gripped him tightly. The room's heavy drapes blocked out the night. "It's weird," she said. "But this reminds me of when we were little kids in a way. Remember how me and you and Amy would just run around in her backyard and how everything was love?" She kissed his shoulder, his hand, his chin.

The motel room spun. Paul freed one of his feet from the covers and placed it on the floor to anchor him. When had it changed? When he was little, God was love. Jesus was love. And the adults all seemed to love one another and him and Rachel and Amy. But soon God became much less about love and more about, well, surveillance. God could see inside your heart, he was told, because your heart belonged to Him. God could see the demons living in your spirit, trying to take you away from Him. God could tell your mother all your secrets and sins because she was closer to God than you and therefore had a right to know. He imagined what his mother already knew about his trip with Rachel, presumably from God.

"God's not love anymore," he said.

"But that's the thing," Rachel said. "That's what I'm trying to say, I guess. God can still be love. We can start from scratch, like Amy did. It can all be love. Just like when we were kids."

She smelled bad, Paul thought. Why hadn't he noticed a few minutes earlier? Desperate for air, he pulled away. When they were teenagers, he remembered, their parents had taken him, Rachel, and Amy, en masse, to a Christian theme park. Some recent scandal involving the evangelist who owned the place had made the tickets cheap. At the theme park—which was plastered everywhere with great banners reading "Forgiven!"—they'd ridden waterslides, visited goats that lived on the property, and attended church services in a vast sanctuary rimmed with television cameras. The park included a shopping mall where Paul, Rachel, and Amy were permitted to walk alone. "Forget Israel," Amy Rotolo had scoffed to Rachel and Paul during one of their walks. "For the Second Coming, Jesus should just show up here." In the daytimes, the teenagers and their parents (though Rachel's father hadn't come) attended workshops about "healing the family." At one point, the kids were told to sit, eyes closed, while their parents stroked their faces. Paul had wanted to scream when he felt his father's hands. Demons, he worried. Afterward, he looked at Amy and Rachel. Rachel's head lay on her mother's shoulder. But Amy sat between her parents, knees hugged to her chest. She was looking at the ground as though in horror.

"Maybe it wasn't ever love," Paul said. "Maybe we just didn't notice."

"Not with our mothers, it wasn't," Rachel agreed. "Not with the church either. But with you and me and Amy and God, it always was. And now it always can be."

What a nice story, he thought. They could live on Rachel's dwindling savings while they built their lives little by little, the past erased except for one golden detail: childhood sweethearts reconciled. But the phrase's magic vanished when he imagined his parents, the Rotolos, and the Bianchis. They were probably congregating at someone's house to pray for him right now, casting out his demons, bemoaning his ingratitude. Mrs. Bianchi would have made a casserole for his mother. His father, meanwhile, would probably be itemizing the comforts they'd given him—the house, the money, the church, the store. It was easy for Rachel, Paul thought. She wasn't obligated to honor anyone.

What could he do? He couldn't possibly return home with Rachel, inhabit his parents' house with her, attend his parents' church with her, let her play mother to his parents' grandchild. He couldn't possibly run away forever with her, either, as though they could build a life from salvaged bits of childhood happiness. They would have to find a new happiness to build on, as Amy possibly had. He recalled a night, years and years ago, before Rachel left for college, when they'd fought in his father's car until Rachel bent his finger back, breaking it. What new happiness was possible for them? Where in the world would it come from?

Paul sat up. His clothes lay in a grubby heap on the floor. He reached for his shirt and pulled it on.

"Paul?"

They looked at one another. One of Rachel's cheeks bore imprints from the bed sheets. They were getting older, the two of them. "Lee told me," she said.

"What?"

"That you love me, don't you? You always have, right?"

He stared at her, trying to figure it out. "I don't know," he said. Once, when Paul was twelve or thirteen years old, he and his father had fought, and though Paul was too old for spankings, his father had struck him across the face. Afterward, the next day, maybe, he'd brought home a little dog, a small spaniel from the mall pet store. Paul had sat beside the puppy's crate, staring at it through the bars. "You can't love anyone," his mother had said to him. "Look at you. You can't even love a dog." Why had this always been so important to everyone? What was so great, so essential, after all, about *his* love?

"I know why you're angry," Rachel said. "You figured out there wasn't an abortion."

"No," Paul said. "I already knew that."

"I wasn't trying to cause trouble. Or, not so much trouble anyway."

"I know."

"You can stay," Rachel said.

He longed, momentarily, for her legs wrapped around him again, for the absolute pleasure of her body against his eclipsing everything else. All consequences, values, and sins would fade to pinpricks, and what was happening could keep happening without any future at all. Then his parents' faces rose in his imagination, and he put his pants on, too.

"You're as bad as Alan," she said, but she didn't sound angry. "Neither of you even cares where they sent me. Neither of you even thought to ask."

Paul shook his head. He'd almost forgotten she'd been sent away. "I'm sorry," he said.

"Well?" Rachel asked. "Didn't you even wonder where I was?"

"No," he admitted. He thought of that miserable theme park, the banners and church services and his father's hands on his face. He thought of his church, the endless Sundays of altar calls, the crisis prayer meetings and exorcisms. He thought of the perpetual fear of being left alone to suffer through the Tribulation which had marked his childhood, and the illustrated version of the End Times story he'd read in Sunday School, which showed an unfathomable earth the day after the Rapture where even animals would forget their place; wild birds would land on people's arms and heads, marauding lions would roam playgrounds, and cats and dogs would turn against their owners. He remembered the nightmares he'd had all through grade school. He remembered how, every morning on his way to school, he worried the streets would be filled with murderous former pets.

Details aside, he thought, he already knew where Rachel went. Wherever it was, he'd been there, too.

"I know it was someplace draconian," he offered.

"Yes, Paul." Her voice was quiet. "It was someplace draconian. And it turns out I went there for you."

"For me," Paul said. Was he angry? "But I didn't make you go there. I didn't tell you to make up some story about an abortion and tell it to my mother. I didn't do any of that."

"But it did something for you after all," Rachel said. "It gave you an out."

"An out?"

"You got in my car and came with me, didn't you? You kissed me tonight. You brought me to this motel."

He stared at his feet. What had they looked like when he was a barefoot child running around in Amy Rotolo's backyard?

"So. You got your out," Rachel continued. "Do you want it or not?"

He imagined going home to his parents, how

they would chastise him endlessly. He imagined his church and the long Sundays of public repentance he'd be sure to suffer through. He thought of Lee, who'd greet him with a wounded little nod, her crazy jealousy newly justified, his parents converted to her side. He thought of Alan, and almost laughed when he imagined Alan as the type who might go so far as to strike him, possibly even in the sanctuary. No. There was no way to fix this.

His mother would know what happened tonight, he reminded himself. Everyone would know. Alan or his mother had probably already announced it. It had probably "been revealed" to one of them during prayer. But not because of God, Paul realized. And not because of one of Alan's manufactured prophecies. They would know because it was obvious.

"All those voices they always hear," Paul said. He felt dizzy and thirsty. "The pastor and Alan and my mother? God and the Devil and all that? And all those demons they see? I know what they are. I just figured it out this second. They're just parts of themselves. The things they want or that they're afraid of, or that they figured out or already knew without realizing it. It's not God. It's not demons. It's just them. That's all it's ever been."

"Don't," said Rachel. "It's not like that. *I* hear God.

Or, not hear, no, but it's like I feel Him. When I pray, I feel His love."

"Not me," Paul said. And he pulled on his socks.

"So, what now?" asked Rachel.

"I don't know," he said again. But he remembered a story Lee had told him, one of her horrible childhood experiences. How often he'd tried to block them out, to pretend they were just tales, because to believe them, really believe them, would have been too much. But this one wasn't as bad as the others. She'd just been placed with a new foster family. It was her first or second night there. She was seven years old and lots of people lived in the house—kids and parents and maybe an aunt or grandparent or someone. But she was the only one who was new. After dinner, the whole family sat in a circle in the living room and played a game in which they passed around a pair of scissors while saying "I pass the scissors closed" or "I pass the scissors open." Lee was supposed to guess when it was correct to say which. She watched the scissors. Sometimes they were closed but the person who passed them said "open." Sometimes they were open but the person who passed them said "closed." She kept the scissors closed. "I pass the scissors closed," she said, and everyone laughed because she had said the wrong thing. This went on awhile. Sometimes she was right and sometimes she was wrong, but she had no idea why until she stopped looking at the scissors and noticed everyone's legs. "Closed" referred to crossed legs and "open" to uncrossed legs. The scissors were a red herring. Lee had laughed when she'd told him this story and he'd laughed too, imagining this little girl, her name spelled like a boy's, staring at the inconsequential scissors, trying to solve the riddle. But it didn't seem funny anymore. It seemed a horrible thing to do to a newly arrived orphan who had started from scratch a dozen times in her life and who already felt as though she did everything wrong.

No, he had no way to fix this, but he could find a way to apologize. He could find a way to face consequences and a way to start from scratch. But not here. Not with Rachel. He didn't believe in God, or sin, or demons. He knew now he never had. But he believed in right and wrong, and he knew what was right. "I bought you a puppy," his father had said. Paul, whose cheek was tender and bruised from his father's hand, had not wanted a puppy. But he tried to love it when his parents told him to because a boy is told whom to love and tries to obey. A man figures it out on his own. And when he does, he tries to do right by those he loves—not because of God or his parents, but because it's what he wants to do.

He thought of his father's disappointed face. He thought of Justine, his small stranger. A man doesn't write his children off as disappointments, he thought. He tries to know them as they are; he tries to find reasons to be proud. A man doesn't let his child stay a stranger. In every state he traveled through on his way back to New Jersey, he decided, he'd buy a stuffed dog to bring home to Justine. No. That was *his* father. He'd get to know the dogs Justine already owned and loved. He'd ask her to show him her favorites, and he'd line them up on her bed and use them to tell her the story of where he went, why he came home, and how sorry he was. And if she cried, he wouldn't walk away.

He didn't know, yet, the dark months that awaited, how he and Lee would soon pack their belongings and move to a small apartment near the beach, Mrs. Rotolo watching them load the rented van through a gap in her curtains. He didn't know that he would begin selling pianos for his father's competitor because half a decade's work experience left him fit for nothing else, nor that Lee would wait weeks before consenting to touch him, saying only, "I didn't really mean for you to go. I didn't think you'd really go." He didn't know that it would happen on Hallowe'en, after sharing a first trick or treat with Justine, her hand in his hand, great felt brown spots, weakly glued to a pair of long johns, falling from the puppy costume Lee had made for her. After he and Justine got home, his daughter's plastic jack-o-lantern teeming with cheap sweets, Lee would look at the ruined costume, and Paul would anticipate Lee's mention of Rachel's name before she could say it, and would pull her close to him instead, kissing her in the hope of staving off that night's bitter quarrel. He didn't know the fight would happen the next night instead and repeat itself, night after night, for months, until he worried their marriage could not survive another evening. He only thought of the canyon and a day—if he had money enough and if Lee and Justine agreed—he might bring them back to Oregon so they could all see it together.

"That canyon thing," he told Rachel. "The thing we saw before dark."

"The Columbia River Gorge," Rachel said. "You asked the bartender, remember?"

He didn't remember. "I think Lee and Justine should see it with me," he said.

"Do you want the car?" she asked.

"Alan's car?"

"It's my car." She looked as though she might cry. "Yours if you want it."

"I don't mean immediately," he said.

"I know." She wrapped herself in the sheet and

moved toward the window to open the drapes. Their room was fairly low to the ground and overlooked two dumpsters in the parking lot.

"It's your car," he said. "You keep it."

"There's a bus station next to the bar where we were. It would probably only take a week to get back."

"Thanks," he said.

"You'll need money."

"Thanks," he repeated. He might never see her again, he realized. "What about you?" he asked.

"That plaque next to Amy's door. It's funny. I never thought about it like that, about having a 'self,' you know?"

"We weren't raised to think that way. We were raised in the way they thought we should go."

"Trained," said Rachel. "The scripture says trained."

"Even worse," said Paul.

"I need to see Amy," Rachel said. "My whole life, you know, it's all you and Amy, too." Her eyes brightened. "Or just Amy now. That's where the love is. Where my 'self' is, I guess. That's where God is for me."

"And after that?"

"I don't know." She smiled at him. "I guess I'll find my way."

Christmas

On the phone, Alan had sounded strange. It was Saturday afternoon, sixteen days before Christmas, and Lou had been working on tomorrow's sermon in his office below the sanctuary. Lou hoped the summer's lingering upheaval would subside or be mitigated by cheer and holly. Tomorrow, the choir would sing "Silent Night" for the first time all season, and next week, they'd perform their annual Christmas Cantata. The nativity had been erected on the altar, and in fifteen days, the candlelight midnight Christmas Eve service would be attended, Lou hoped, by all the parishioners—those who came regularly and those who didn't, women in green velvet dresses, their hair pulled back, their necklines revealing collarbone, or cleavage, or buttery shoulders. He was an old man, and women no longer gazed at him the way they once had, but they touched him more than they used to, at Christmas especially.

He could have been a different kind of pastor, one of those charismatic evangelists who preached righteousness every Sunday morning, then culled a new mistress from the congregation—sometimes married, sometimes not—every Sunday afternoon. Some of the guys he'd graduated Bible school with had become pastors like that; some even had churches ten times the size of his. He'd had those opportunities, those temptations, over the years. When Kathleen, in her forties, still hadn't given him a living son, he'd meditated on Abraham and the barren Sarah and understood Abraham's sin of going to Hagar. Every so often, when a young woman would come to his office alone, he'd feel tempted by the opportunity. But he'd always stayed appropriate and chaste. God hadn't promised him a son, he'd remind himself. That promise was Abraham's. Lou's calling was to have a church instead. Even as a boy, newly arrived in America with his mother and father a few years after Mussolini's death, he'd wanted to be a priest. He learned his catechism, served as an altar boy, took his confirmation. Then the family moved from Trenton, New Jersey, where they'd initially settled, to Riverview, which was then a little town in the country with cheap land owned by lots of Italians and an occasional Irish, and a solid Roman Catholic Church. Lou's parents played cards at the Italian American Club, Lou's father opened a barber shop, and Lou and his brothers and sisters made friends with their nearest neighbors, an Irish family called Brennan, the youngest of whom, pretty Kathleen—never Kate or Katie or Kathy—would one day, much to his parents' chagrin (there were Italian girls everywhere, they told him) become his bride. Priests couldn't marry, of course, so after marrying Kathleen, Lou worked in his father's barber shop, cutting hair.

Kathleen got pregnant twice. The first time, the baby died inside her, just died four months before he was meant to be born. They christened him Louis Junior. The second time, Lou told Kathleen to quit her job at the florist. He told her to lie down. He cooked for her—old recipes he'd learned from his mother and taught his Irish wife to love. Sometimes, the priest from St. Joseph's would come to visit because Lou didn't want Kathleen to exert herself by going to church. He only wanted her to rest. But that baby died, too. "It was God's will," the priest said, but Lou couldn't fathom why it would be. Then, in his late thirties, still grieving his dead children, Lou heard some of the college-age Catholics at his church talk about making a pilgrimage to Explo, a Christian summer festival in Dallas, and he and Kathleen went. They'd never had a proper honeymoon, they reasoned.

Explo was unlike anything he'd ever seen. They were nearly two full decades older than a lot of the kids there—some were hippie kids calling themselves Jesus Freaks, who looked poor although they hadn't been raised that way, and others looked like him and Kathleen—"nickeys," the Jesus Freaks called them. Billy Graham preached, and at the end of the festival, Johnny Cash sang to them—hundreds of thousands of them—at the Cotton Bowl. "I want to start a church," he told Kathleen. "A living church like this. It will be our child." Two years later, at the brand new Oklahoma Bible school named for the Word of God itself, Lou met other men who'd decided to start ministries at Explo. But most of them talked about hearing God's voice, loud and clear, calling them to do it. "I had a very quiet calling," he would sometimes say, almost apologetically. And it took him years of prayer and study before he believed he could actually hear the voice of God.

When he graduated from Bible school, he and Kathleen moved back to Riverview. The town had grown, but the vestigial members of the One Way Movement still attended St. Joseph's. Lou and Kathleen befriended them—they were young, married kids with long hair and babies. Kathleen and Lou were almost like parents to them. The church was born in Lou and Kathleen's rented house on Vaughn Avenue where, every Friday night, they held prayer meetings the kids attended with their babies and tambourines and dirty feet. Now those kids were in their late forties, their babies were in their mid-twenties, and Lou was sixty-two. "The days of our years are threescore years and ten," he often reminded himself. He could see it from here, the end of the lifespan God had promised.

He was an old man, eight years from seventy, but he still loved Christmas, the sight of all the raised candles in the darkened sanctuary, the smell of burning wax, the overdressed children asleep in the pews, heads on their mothers' thighs. Tomorrow was the last of the special pre-holiday collections, and because Alan had been given the job to pray over the collection plates before they were passed around the congregation, Lou had wanted to meet with him to plan what he would say. Lou was afraid he'd give too much information—the costs of the extra holiday services and egregious salaries requested by the choir director and soloists who'd come all the way from Manhattan. Lou didn't want the congregation to know. Nothing curtailed generosity like a list of expenses. And, in recent months, the collection plates had yielded less and less. Lou was a man of God, it was true, but he was a businessman, too. He knew it was no time to make mistakes.

But when he'd called Alan, asking him to meet him

in his office, Alan had answered stiffly, "You know what? I'm hungry. Let's meet for lunch instead" and he'd suggested the local Italian-style chain, a place with food so inauthentic that Kathleen always referred to it as "that American restaurant." Poor Alan, Lou thought; he always tried so hard.

"You all right?" Lou had asked. Always before, Alan would have foregone a hundred meals to meet with the pastor.

"I don't know," Alan had answered, and Lou had heard his voice break.

"Satan has been on the warpath these last months," Lou had said.

And Alan had answered, "I'll see you at 1:00."

Lou arrived at the restaurant a little before 1:00. Riverview had so many franchise restaurants; when he'd first moved back after Bible school, trees still lined most roads. But within ten years of the mall being built on one side of the highway, dozens of strip malls had raised their concrete heads on the other. Now, big box warehouse retailers colonized the street, and among those cinderblock buildings sat restaurant after restaurant—steakhouses and rib joints and seafood chains and franchise buffets. The park behind the highway where the church had always held its picnics had changed too. It still had a large empty field, perfect for setting up barbecue grills, but the forest that had once ringed the field was gone. Years ago, when the families would arrive, they'd park on the other side of the trees and emerge from the forest like enchanted creatures, the wives carrying armloads of paper plates and covered dishes of beans or spareribs or homemade cookies, the men bearing the weight of large coolers of ice and bottled soda. From the shadows of the trees, Eddie Esposito and his bocce set would emerge and the kids would chase the heavy, hard balls when the men threw them into the grass. The musicians would bring their acoustic guitars and they'd all stay in the park late into the night, holding the evening service among the trees, mosquito-repelling candles burning. These days, without the trees, from the field you could see the gray tops of the highway stores and hear the sighing traffic, and the picnics were short when they occurred. No one seemed to bring guitars anymore. Fewer Italians attended the church too, it seemed. No one but the older men knew how to play bocce.

Alan hadn't arrived yet, but as it was lunchtime on a Saturday near Christmas, the restaurant was crowded and no tables were available. Lou gave his name to the hostess and waited on a wooden bench in the foyer. All these restaurants smelled the same, he thought, like hot water and yeast. Christmas trees stood in every corner. They were all the same too, artificial, dark green, decorated with white lights and red bows. Secular Christmas carols played over the loudspeaker and the other restaurant guests looked as though their backs ached from shopping. He and Kathleen didn't shop at malls anymore. Occasionally, they would walk at the senior shopping center before it opened in the mornings, but when they had to buy things, they ordered from catalogs over the telephone.

They were slowing down, he and Kathleen. And this had been a hard year. Funny how hard years can wear on you when you're old, Lou thought. He'd had hard years when he was young and living among immigrants with his parents and siblings, and even harder ones when he and Kathleen had lost their babies, but today's hardships felt heavier somehow. When you're young, he thought, years are yours to waste. Easy, hard, it didn't matter; a year was only something to dispense with as quickly as possible so the next one could come. It was different now. When you're old, he thought, the harder the year, the higher its cost.

And things had been hard ever since the church had built that colossal sanctuary on the highway. The building was expensive to keep and the church's infrastructure required constant attention. When he was younger, hosting Bible studies for thirty folks in his living room on Friday nights, the interior narrative of his days had mostly to do with building the church—his wife and those lost babies too, of course, but mostly building the church. But the church had been built for many years, so his thoughts largely focused on its economic maintenance. He worried over salaries for the church's schoolteachers in the face of declining enrollments, the electric and water bills, and the upkeep the facility always seemed to require. He worried about the wireless microphones that seemed to falter into uselessness every week, the printer in the office that had started spitting paper back out as confetti, the plush toys in the pre-school that needed to be replaced after the last bout of lice, the floor in the downstairs men's bathroom that seemed to be sinking into the foundation, the termites that had been spotted in the choir's rehearsal room. If they were there, Lou reasoned, they were everywhere. What was worse, over the last few months, church attendance had declined; people had been rattled. Their faith had been disrupted. If attendance didn't pick up soon, there would be financial troubles too terrible to contemplate.

Never had his church known a time of greater

tribulation than it had in these recent months. In late summer, he'd sent Rachel, Alan's wife and one of the younger generation, away because she'd confessed to having had an abortion nearly a decade earlier. The thirty and younger crowd fell away a bit because of that—not because of the abortion, he'd heard second-hand, but because of Lou's response. They'd sympathized with Rachel, who'd refused to stay at the ministry to which he'd sent her and had come home just long enough to pick up her belongings. Unfortunately, she'd also picked up Eddie Esposito's son, Paul, another young man from the church who, not incidentally, was someone else's husband. Rachel still hadn't returned, but Paul had come back in September, had quit his job, quit the church, and had stopped talking to his own parents. Apparently, Paul's wife had taken him back, but she'd stopped coming to church, too. They'd relinquished their house to Paul's parents and had moved to an apartment across the bridge. On Hallowe'en, Alan had reportedly been walking through the poorer neighborhoods, giving out tracts, and he saw Paul and his daughter, Justine. They were trick or treating. It was an activity the church specifically prohibited. Justine was dressed as a puppy, Alan said.

And somehow, the news of their departures must

have ricocheted through the younger congregants, winnowing out what seemed like dozens. The older men and women, Lou's contemporaries or longtime friends, would always remain loyal, but members of the church's younger generations were disappearing. The scandal had served as the catalyst, but Lou knew the young folks' exodus was attributable to more than that. Jesus just wasn't cool anymore. No, Lou corrected himself. Jesus had never been cool, not even when Lou had led those prayer meetings and had started the church, but *Lou* had been cool then, able to connect. He'd known the kinds of jokes to tell, the kinds of analogies to draw. He'd known how to talk to young people. But he'd forgotten. He was too tired or too old or he'd just lost the ability to keep up.

He had no children, he told himself again and again; he'd raised a church instead. He didn't want it to grow old and to die with its pastor, as so many churches did. The youth needed to come back. This was why, in part, he'd delegated the task of praying over the collection to Alan. It was a flashy little job, twenty minutes long, a mini-sermon. Usually, he commissioned one of the church's elders. But Alan was young, and better yet, had survived the scandal without losing his faith. He wasn't the perfect spokesman—he was naive and slightly dim, but he was charismatic and full of fire, and a better choice than some of the other remaining young people, all of whom seemed crippled by a lack of faith, or maybe confidence. That was part of the problem, Lou reflected. In the younger folks, it was hard to tell the difference between faith and confidence.

Alan entered the restaurant just when the hostess called, "Lou, party of two." He looked thinner than usual, Lou noticed, and his eyes seemed swollen. Lou thought of a story he could tell Alan, an illustrative anecdote that one of the teachers from Bible school had told Lou and the other students long ago. One day, early in his ministry, the man claimed to have woken up with one eye gummed closed. He heard the voice of Satan declare, "You're going to preach today with one eye shut." But the man had cast Satan away. Afterward, he'd soaked his eye under a warm compress, it had opened as though nothing had ever been wrong, and that morning, fifty-four people were saved at his church. Lou would never forget that story or its moral, which he knew he should relay to Alan today: "The closer you get to God, the closer the Devil comes. This is the time to be strong in the Lord. Hallelujah."

But Alan didn't ask for an anecdote. He simply looked at Lou and said, "I'm starving," and they followed the hostess to a table.

First, a waiter brought a basket of yeasty bread, too soft to be genuinely Italian. Alan broke a piece from the loaf. A flask of imitation olive oil sat in the center of the table. Alan poured a small puddle of it onto his bread plate and dusted the puddle with parmesan cheese. How Kathleen would laugh, Lou thought, at this oil so pale it was practically yellow and at the parmesan cheese in a glass shaker instead of Romano cheese grated fresh. But Alan dipped his bread into the mixture and ate. His lips shone.

"Alan," Lou said. "We need to talk about what you're going to say tomorrow."

Alan only took another piece of bread, dipped it in the paste of oil and cheese and said, "I don't think I can do it, Pastor Lou." He chewed and swallowed, as though to buy time. Then he said, "I don't think I can come to your church anymore."

Years ago, Lou would have known what to say. He would have known how to turn this into a teaching that would have persuaded Alan not only to come to church, but exactly what appeal would best have worked for the congregation. Things were beginning to slip from him, though. He was tired.

He, too, broke a piece of bread from the loaf and chewed. It was warm and soft, like a woman's thigh.

He wanted, briefly, to be a young man again, to live forever as a young man. Then, just as briefly, he wanted to die, to never again endure another day as someone old. "Alan." It was all he could think to say.

Alan looked down at his plate.

Lou reached across the table and clasped Alan's wrist with both hands. The waiter arrived with their salad bowls and more bread, looked at Lou's hands, and said, "I'll give you a few more minutes," at which Lou had wanted to laugh. It seemed like television, Lou thought, those shows young people liked, shows with the one-line jokes that sounded like mocking. That was why he couldn't keep the young people's attention from the pulpit nowadays, he decided. He didn't even understand what they watched on TV.

"I started my own group," Alan said. "At my house. Every week."

"Alan," Lou said again.

The waiter returned. Lou let go of Alan's wrist and ordered spaghetti marinara. The sauce would be terrible, Lou knew, full of sugar and acid. He tried to remember the way his mother's spaghetti sauce tasted. She'd make it special every Sunday, when they'd eat dinner in the afternoon, shortly after getting home from Mass. But he couldn't remember. He was an old man, he told himself. He remembered less and less.

"It's what the Lord told me to do," Alan said.

"But what about your theology?" Lou asked. He felt a flash of irritation. Alan worked in office supplies, for goodness sake. "Where will you get ordained?"

"There's no time for that," Alan answered. "Look at this." From his pocket, he procured a wrinkled newspaper photograph of a lanky, sandy-haired man. "You know about him?"

The caption indicated the man would run for a state congressional seat in the next mid-term election. Lou had never heard of him; it wasn't the kind of political office the news deemed important enough for prominent reports. He couldn't even begin to pronounce the man's endlessly long name which began with the improbable combination of letters "Hjo."

"Pastor," Alan said. "We're at the End Times, and it's my generation that needs to lead. The Lord tells me things. I know things about this man."

Threescore and ten, Lou reminded himself. He had no sons. Only the church would succeed him. "What?" he asked. "What could you possibly know?"

Their entrees came. It was too fast, Lou decided. The food couldn't be fresh. He twirled his spaghetti around his fork and blew steam away before eating. It all tasted like tap water.

"You didn't say grace," Alan said.

Lou shuddered as though he'd been caught stealing. "I said it before you came," he offered. But he knew Alan was leaving him, leaving the church, one more young person gone.

"This is the Antichrist," Alan said, indicating the picture again. "He might win. And from there, he'll go for higher offices. The Lord called me to start an army, here on the ground."

"An army?" the pastor asked. The spaghetti was overcooked. "It's like a bloodworm," Kathleen would say. "Like the bait your father must have used when he fished back in the Old Country."

"They've been coming to my house," Alan said again. "They're young, Pastor Lou. They're like radicals. Totally on fire for God. And more come every week, just like God said they would."

Lou had always known Alan was gullible, but that gullibility, before, had always seemed a blessing. It was the gullibility of a child about whom Jesus Himself might have said, "Suffer the little children to come unto Me." But to believe the Lord had called him to start an army? To identify the Antichrist from a newspaper photograph? To believe that the Bible's prophecies somehow could be interpreted to include Riverview, New Jersey? He tried to keep his voice calm. "Check it against your spirit, Alan," he said. "Are you sure you're hearing God?"

Alan nodded. "It's crazy, right? That voice of truth? That voice that always talks to me?" He pushed his soup bowl away like a child. "Of course it's God," he said.

"Listen," Lou began. He wanted to tell Alan about the mistakes he'd made earlier in his own ministry, the times he'd thought he'd heard God's voice when he hadn't. He wanted to remind Alan of the time he thought he'd been told to resurrect Rachel's mother. That incident more than anything else, Lou decided, probably undermined her faith. "Have you talked to Rachel at all?" he asked. "It's been a terrible year for you."

"It has nothing to do with Rachel," Alan said, blinking. "I'm the one who's leaving."

"The church needs you," the pastor said. But he noticed Alan gazing into his lap, unconvinced. "If you want leadership, I could consider making you an elder. The youngest elder the church has ever had." But Alan refused to look up. "Come on, Alan. Don't be ridiculous."

"It *is* ridiculous," Alan agreed. "I've been thinking that a lot. Loyalty to a pastor. To a church. How a pastor can become a kind of idol? You told me Rachel would come back, that she wouldn't be gone long, and I listened to you. I waited for weeks like you told me to. I followed you. But it's the End Times. And I have to follow Jesus."

"You've had a terrible year," Lou said again. And he knew what to say next, knew how to reach Alan the way he used to know how to reach everyone. "You need healing. You're too susceptible to Satan's lies. You've been through too much. It's made you angry with God. But that's a sin, Alan. It's an opening for the Devil. And he's been watching you, waiting for that opening for years, waiting for the chance to get his claws in. What you're talking about, this army of yours, it's fortune-telling. It's charlatanism."

Alan shook his head. "Charlatans and fortune-tellers are liars. I'm not."

Lou contemplated putting his hands on Alan's head to cast out his demons right here at the restaurant, but he felt too old, too tired for theatrics away from the pulpit. The Lord had given free will. *Of course you're a charlatan,* he wanted to say. *Without a single year of theological study, you're starting a militaristic church to oppose a two-bit local politician you think is the Antichrist?* But instead, he said, "You watch too much TV."

"I don't have a TV," Alan answered. "You told us

not to have them and I obeyed you. I always obeyed you." He wiped his hands on a napkin and stood. "Thank you," he said, extending one of his newly wiped hands to the pastor. Lou took it. It was a large hand, rough and dry.

"My father hated me," Alan said. "But when I was hungry, you fed me. I was thirsty and you gave me drink. I was a stranger and you took me in. I was naked and you clothed me."

"Inasmuch as I have done it for the least of you," Lou continued, picking up the end of the scripture, "I did it for the Lord." One day, he would remember nothing but the scriptures. The thought gave him peace.

Alan laid a fifty dollar bill on the table. It was enough to cover the price of lunch more than three times over.

What would Lou say in service tomorrow? Everyone would notice Alan's absence. How could this newest and most significant departure be taught? The congregation's few remaining young people would leave once they heard. They'd lose their faith entirely or they'd flee to Alan's crazy End Times boot camp. Some of them probably already had. The pasta had disappeared from Lou's plate. How had that happened? He didn't remember having eaten it all. He wished for so many meals to eat again, so many meals he ate without noticing. He watched the shoppers at neighboring tables. They struggled with their bags.

Mission work, Lou decided as he helped himself to Alan's uneaten soup. It was terrible, too salty, too diluted. He would tell the church that, as a Christmas present, he'd sent Alan on mission work. It had always been Alan's heart's desire, he would say. He would announce it just before the collection; it might even get people to kick in extra. And if any of Alan's little disciples dared to appear in service, if they dared to contradict him, he would cast out their demons in front of everyone to punish them for playing fortune-telling games with a fake pastor. He was an old man, he had no sons, and this was his beloved church. It would succeed him when he died.

CORRINA WYCOFF is the author of the novel-in-stories, *O Street*, and her fiction and essays have appeared in journals, magazines, and anthologies. She lives in Washington State where she teaches English at Pierce College.